SHADOW GAME

Shadow Alliance Series

SHAWNA COLEING

Free Novella

GET the novella *Shadow Alliance* free

Simply by signing up for the (no-spam) newsletter, I'll send you the prequel to the Shadow Alliance Series - Find out more at the end of the book.

Chapter 1

THE SOFT LIGHT from the full moon concealed the cancerous blemishes of an old fishing boat as it chugged through the smooth waters of the Mediterranean.

The beguiling sea was quiet on this particular night. Its dark depths allowed safe travel to all who passed over. But not for long.

Within the boat, a wiry-looking man with a strong back and wary eyes washed his hands in the rusty sink. He ran his wet fingers through his hair to smooth it. It had been a long time since Arthur had been this long on a boat, and his expectation that it would be like riding a bike was accurate enough. He found his sea legs quickly and discovered that despite the possible treacherous circumstances — or perhaps because of them — he was enjoying this mission more than the others that had come before.

He observed his reflection in the chipped mirror and scratched at the stubble on his face, then went back to his bunk.

In another part of the ship, the captain, Marco Santores, snorted awake and sat bolt upright, ducking his head to avoid hitting it on the board above.

He rubbed a hand on his bulging stomach, the source of the harbinger that alerted him to the fact that something wasn't right.

Rolling out of bed, he pulled on a grubby shirt that fit too loose in some spots and too tight in others, then exited his room.

After hauling himself up the wooden ladder, the captain entered the wheelhouse, slapping his first mate's dirty boots off the console. "Pater. Why have we slowed?"

Pater grunted and lifted himself out of the captain's chair. "What do you expect to get out of her? The engine's struggling. That's all."

"She doesn't give in that easy." Marco checked the dials and was about to tell off his incompetent employee when the humming engine hardened into a clank.

His lips slammed shut as he spun and yanked hard on the bell, rousing the crew.

The engineer woke from a fitful dream, glad to be rid of the nightmare until he registered the new sounds coming from below deck and wasn't sure if he'd awakened into another one.

After stuffing his feet into his unlaced boots, he bowed his way through the small passages and down a ladder to find water filling the engine room.

"*Guaio!*" he shouted to anyone who could hear above and rang his own bell.

The captain soon filled the small doorway and made

the sign of the cross. "Robby," he called across the clamoring motor. "The bilge pumps."

The engineer glared back at his captain as he traversed the greasy waters of the trespassing sea. "Where do you think I'm going?"

The captain turned and went back up on deck, passing Arthur on the way. "Be ready," he said, slapping his passenger on the back. "We may need to abandon ship."

Arthur dropped the small box he was holding into his satchel as he watched Marco go, then he slipped down below and found the engineer spewing out foul words to match the filth that surrounded him.

"What is it?" Arthur yelled out above the din.

"The bilge pump. Someone's destroyed it." Robby waded back through the deepening water toward Arthur. "We have to alert the captain. The ship is lost."

Arthur stepped down onto the top rung. "I can tell him."

"There's nothing more I can do here," Robby said as he reached the ladder.

A muffled clang reverberated through the small space just before the engine sputtered and died.

Crew members were lowering a life raft into the water when the ship lurched and Arthur stumbled over the thick rope on deck.

Marco appeared beside him from the wheelhouse. "Get in the raft, just in case," the captain said as his eyes darted to each crew member. "Robby's still below?"

He didn't wait for an answer before he turned to check on his remaining crew member.

Arthur grabbed his beefy arm. "Robby said the bilge isn't working. We'll have to abandon ship."

Marco nodded and turned.

Arthur grabbed him again. "What about the cargo?"

The captain looked around the boat and stated what he considered to be an obvious fact. "I'm sorry, lad. But your medical supplies are lost."

Arthur bobbed his head in assent, then pinched his lips together as he watched the captain go to find his missing engineer.

There was nothing more for Arthur to do here. His job was done now that all the loose ends had been tied up, so he joined the rest of the crew in the raft.

It wasn't long before Marco's head appeared from above, his face grim. He counted the men below before climbing down into the raft.

"Shove off." His voice was barely above a whisper.

"But, Captain."

"I said, shove off." The anger that burst forth didn't match the pain in his eyes.

"We're not leaving without Robby," asserted one of the crew.

Marco bowed his head. "Robby's gone. I can't figure it except that he hit his head and fell in the water and drowned. He'd want to be buried by the sea. Let's go."

Chapter 2

OLIVER DUG his thumb into his shoulder, wincing at the resulting burn, but he continued to prod until the spasm retreated. He'd already swallowed a couple of painkillers but it would take time for the familiar discomfort to ease enough for him to go back to sleep.

His phone lit up on the glass coffee table in front of him, then scooted across the surface as it vibrated. Oliver scooped it up, his pain momentarily forgotten.

"Arthur?"

"Oliver, I'm glad you're awake."

"I take it everything has arrived safely?"

"I'm sorry, but I have bad news."

Over the past several weeks, Oliver had been over all the worst-case scenarios and finally put them to rest, but those words brought every one of them screaming back into a new possible reality. All he could do was wait silently until Arthur continued.

"The boat didn't make it to Libya. It sank."

Oliver lifted the phone from the side of his face and

touched the edge to his forehead before bringing it back to his ear. "But you're safe?"

"I am."

"And the crew? Was anyone hurt?"

"We lost one. The engineer. Seems he had an accident when the boat was taking on water."

Oliver closed his eyes and stood. "Find out about his family. I want them compensated."

"It's my understanding that he had no next of kin."

"There must be someone!" Oliver squeezed the bridge of his nose. "I'm sorry. I don't mean to yell. You've been through enough already." His gaze ran across the thousands of twinkling lights filling the city below.

"Don't worry about me. But, Oliver, the cargo was lost."

"I expected that. But what about the *other* cargo?"

"That's what I was referring to."

Oliver let that new information settle like a lump in the pit of his stomach before responding. "You're still in Libya, I take it?"

"Yes. I've organized to fly out later today. I'm sorry, Oliver."

"I'm just glad you're safe. Get in touch when you're back. And try to get some rest."

"Thanks, Oli."

After Oliver hung up the phone, he tossed it onto the couch, then looked down at his shoulder, the pain of which paled in comparison to what he now suffered.

He knew Captain Marco personally and had been

assured that the boat could easily make the journey. Even the weather reports had looked good.

Pressing the heels of his hands into his eyes, he exhaled a sharp breath. The consequences of this outcome were too devastating to comprehend at the moment.

He kept his eyes squeezed tightly shut, but when his world began shrinking to the size of the inside of a box, they snapped open. Revisiting the past was more than he could handle tonight.

He entered the kitchen and slipped a mug under the coffee maker. But as the brew filled the cup, he found the smell curdling in his stomach and the coffee remained untouched. He opted instead for a quick swig of water from under the faucet before moving again to stand in front of the large window with its magnificent city views. It was a stark contrast to the troubled uncertainty he now felt. His eyes lifted to the dark sky, and he shook his head.

"I was so sure it was the right move." He sucked his bottom lip into his mouth and bit it. How could he have gotten it so wrong?

───────

Morgan's rubber soles slapped softly on the cold concrete. It was a sound she was hearing for the last time and strange to think she'd miss it. No, *miss* was the wrong word. It was more like the dripping tap you get used to, but when the sound is gone, you're still relieved. The problem was, she didn't feel relieved.

After three years in prison for a crime she didn't commit, Morgan was walking out a free woman after new evidence emerged and she was exonerated. But the money she received from her wrongful incarceration didn't compensate for the fact that everything she had worked so hard to create had crumbled to dust because she had been locked away.

She'd leave prison with a small nest egg, but that couldn't restore her reputation. Even in innocence, she knew she'd be forever tainted by her stint in prison. She shuffled along, and her lips puckered when it occurred to her that it was true in more ways than one. She had always had a hard edge, but her years in prison had sharpened it to a fine point. Everything she was taking away from here was worse than nothing.

She fingered the letter in her pocket. Well, not everything.

The guard put a hand up to stop her and Morgan waited behind the line for the door to unlock.

She wouldn't have to do that anymore either.

While she waited for her paperwork to be completed, she slipped her hand into the pocket of her jumpsuit again and pulled out the letter.

Most inmates communicated by email, but having been arrested for computer fraud, she hadn't been allowed access to the computers, and instead had exchanged letters with her old high school friend, Camilla, who had assured Morgan she'd be there to pick her up when she was released.

. . .

It was another hour before everything was completed and she could change into the only clothes she now had: baggy jeans and a black tee-shirt with a giant panda face on it.

Finally, she collected a personal item she'd been without since being locked up, a rose-gold ring with a heart that she now slipped onto her index finger. Then she tucked her brown hair behind her ear and lifted her bag off the floor before taking an inaudible breath.

As she was escorted out of the prison, her heart squeezed tighter with each step that brought her closer to her unexpected freedom.

Camilla Hargrave, a slim blonde with piles of wavy blond hair and a very short skirt, waved excitedly from the side of an aging Cadillac before racing toward Morgan, who increased her grip on the bag she was carrying. She hadn't seen Camilla in almost ten years.

"You got my letter," Camilla squealed as she grabbed Morgan in a suffocating embrace. Morgan couldn't remember the last time she had been hugged, and she was glad Camilla couldn't see the grimace on her face. If it weren't for her, Morgan would still be locked up, so she forced herself to lift her free arm and pat her friend on the back in reciprocation.

Camilla finally let go and pushed her friend back but

kept her hands clamped on her arms. "Look at you. How long has it been?"

"Well, tenth grade. How long ago was that?"

"Not as long as it feels. I hope."

"You look good," Morgan offered, trying to push the attention off herself.

"You think so?" Camilla said, finally letting Morgan go. She pushed the side of her cheek back. "No wrinkles yet, at least."

Morgan attempted a friendly chuckle, but it came out sounding more like a strangled cat. "Thanks for all of this. I mean, everything."

"Oh, it's nothing." Camilla said, slipping her arm through Morgan's.

"It's not nothing,"

Camilla had contacted Morgan after seeing her on the local news being carted off to prison. They exchanged letters and phone calls. Morgan had refused visits, unable to come to terms with the shame she felt stuck behind bars. It was Camilla who encouraged Morgan — relentlessly — to find a way to prove her innocence after Morgan had finally relented and told her the whole story.

"Water under the bridge. So," Camilla said, leading Morgan to the car, "how's it feel?"

Morgan squinted up at the hazy July sky. "Hot."

"That's not what I mean. How's it feel to be free?"

"I don't know. It doesn't really feel like anything yet. Maybe it will sink in later."

When they got close to the Cadillac, Camilla let go

of Morgan's arm and scurried to open the door. "Your carriage awaits, m'lady."

"I didn't know you had a car."

"Oh, it's not mine. It's my mom's."

"That was nice of her to let you borrow it."

Camilla snorted. "She's passed out on the couch. She won't even know it's gone. We'll have to drop it off before we go home — " Camilla slapped her hand across her mouth. "Home. You're going home. That must feel amazing."

"I'm sure it will, but like I said, it hasn't really sunk in yet."

"Right. But it will. Don't worry. I'll make sure."

"So … I haven't seen your mom in a long time. She probably won't even recognize me."

Camilla snorted again. "I'd rather she didn't even know we were there. Once we ditch the car, there's a bus stop near her place that can take us into the city. Then tomorrow, I've got a little surprise."

Morgan tensed. "What is it?"

"If I told you, it wouldn't be a surprise."

"I don't think I'm up for surprises."

"Oh, you have to be for this one. You'll like it, I promise. Then I'll take you into work the next day."

"I start work in two days?"

"Yeah, we're short-staffed, so the timing is perfect."

Morgan frowned. "I still don't understand why you're doing all of this for me."

"You mean besides what you did for me at school? That was huge. I've owed you for years."

"I wouldn't call standing up to one bully huge."

"Are you kidding? They were all afraid of you. You were an unknown quantity to them. All those dark clothes and foster-care hopping — Hey, you don't still wear black all the time, do you?"

"It's been prison-wear for me for the past three years and this shirt was supplied to me."

Camilla's shoulders dropped in a long sigh. "Thank goodness. Don't go back there. It's terrible for your coloring. Anyway, those girls at school thought you were one whisker shy of losing it and nobody wanted to be the poor soul who was in the firing line, literally. As long as I stuck close to you, they left me alone. No more picking on the trailer-park trash."

"That wasn't why they picked on you. You were prettier and had developed faster than them. They were jealous. But that was a long time ago."

"So?"

"So, a lot has changed since then. I've changed. How do you even know you can trust me?"

"I am an excellent judge of character, and I'm desperate for a new housemate. I told you I can't afford my place without one."

"So you only want me for my money?" Morgan grinned.

Camilla laughed, a tinkling sound Morgan had forgotten. "Absolutely. You know me. Gold digger through and through."

Camilla continued to chatter nonstop until they pulled

14

into the dirt drive in front of her mom's trailer. Several plant pots full of weeds were lined up out front.

"I'll slip the keys into her purse and then we can get home."

Morgan leaned against the hood while Camilla tiptoed up the stairs to the small porch and put an exaggerated shushing finger to her lips as she opened the screen before tucking through the door.

Across the park was a sad attempt at a playground. Sand had been dumped on the ground with no boundaries, which meant most of it was scattered. A kid with a buzz cut and cutoff jean shorts sat on the rusty swing. He was staring at Morgan while pushing himself back and forth, his toes digging into the dirt. His eyebrows lifted every time the chain squealed.

Morgan made a growly face at him, but he wasn't deterred, so she gave in and moved around to the other side of the car where she was blocked from his view.

A screaming yelp blasted from inside the trailer followed by what sounded like glass shattering.

"Mom!" Camilla said. "It's no big deal."

Morgan leaped up the metal grated steps but stopped just short of revealing herself. She was unsure if she should intervene.

"I always knew you were a dirty rotten thief."

Morgan had only met Camilla's mom a couple of times. She was always polite but uninterested, and Camilla believed she was nicest when she was drunk. Morgan wasn't so sure, especially when her friend came to school with bruises, but Morgan was no stranger to abuse and they had always avoided voicing the obvious to each other.

Camila stormed out, nearly colliding with Morgan, who jumped back down to the ground before Camilla slammed the door behind her. The effect was minimal as the screen slapped against the frame with a flat crack and bounced.

"Let's get out of here."

"Did I get you in trouble?" Morgan asked, trying to catch up. It was not a great start to her new life.

Camilla raged at the sky as she steamed across the rocky path. The boy on the swing stopped moving and watched. Camilla turned to him and screamed, "What!"

He stuck his tongue out at her and started swinging again.

Camilla stomped toward the bus stop but paused when they reached the road. She lifted her arms into the air and took a deep breath. Then she lowered her arms as she let it out.

She looked at Morgan and smiled as though nothing had happened. "I'm glad that's over. Let's go have some fun."

Chapter 3

OLIVER STOOD at the head of the conference table, gripping the edge. The six other men and women sat quietly until one man cleared his throat.

"Oliver, we have other matters that need to be dealt with today." Oliver was staring at a smudge in the polished wood and didn't respond. No one at the table had agreed with his decision to send the boat, although they had gone along with it. "If we don't act on the Syrian deal, we'll miss it."

Oliver slapped his hand on the table. "Carl, I will not be responsible for weaponizing the Syrians."

Carl's lips pinched. "I thought I had explained — "

"Don't patronize me. I'm not a boy anymore, and I refuse to be played. The Syrian deal does not line up with the ethos of this company."

Carl indulged in an eye roll. "The ethos of this company? Listen to yourself. It's not our responsibility to ask lots of questions and second-guess everyone's motives. We are simply the middlemen." He waved a half-hearted hand toward one of the women in the room. "And women."

Oliver looked up at the ceiling. "I can't believe you just said that. Of course it's our responsibility. We're not animals."

"And that's not what we're saying." Another of the men spoke up. He had white hair, a dark mustache, and was almost twice Oliver's age. "But when I worked with your father on these deals, he understood the risks and knew when to stay out of it and let people get on with their own affairs. It's how he grew this business into what it is today."

"Brian, I appreciate your commitment to this company, but I am not my father who trusted no one and only cared about the bottom line."

Carl spoke again. "That doesn't change the fact that you are going to have to accept that the shipment was lost and we have to keep moving forward. You don't want to do the Syrian deal? Fine. There are plenty of other opportunities, but you know how it is. You can't take these things personally."

"If I may," a man said from the door. "We all know the consequences of what's just happened, and I do believe Oliver is entitled to take it somewhat personally."

"Arthur." Oliver went to his friend and took one hand in both of his, clasping tightly. "I'm so glad you're okay."

"I'm just sorry I wasn't able to do more."

"No. I don't think I would have been able to bear it if you'd lost your life trying to rescue *things*."

"But they aren't just *things*, are they? They would have saved lives." He addressed the room again. "We might not have all agreed with the profit margin on this job — "

"What profit margin?" someone mumbled.

"But a successful business isn't always about profit. People want to be associated with a company that cares about others and is seen to be at least trying to do good in the world."

"Arthur's right," said a plain-looking, middle-aged woman with straight brown hair. "We should support Oliver."

"No one here has a problem with these philanthropic assignments, Eve," said another woman with her blond hair pulled back into a bun. "The problem we have is how they're carried out. Everyone knows the Mediterranean is a dangerous body of water to cross. And just because some sea captain in a rickety ship looking to put coin in his pocket says his boat can cross the sea, despite these countless boats that don't make it, why do we take his word over the Syrians?"

"I wish I could explain it to you so you could understand," Oliver said with a heavy sigh.

"You had better start learning how quickly, because we're getting fed up with your schemes," said Carl.

Oliver's hands pressed into the top of the table, creating a halo around his fingertips. "Is that a threat?"

"Of course not, but Oliver, you need to see it from our perspective. We want to stand beside you, but we have no idea what you are doing or why."

"So the entire problem here stems from my inadequate communication skills. Fine, then let's move on to something you will understand. Otherwise we'll be here all day and get nothing done."

He sat down and pulled his chair in, linking his fingers in front of him. He felt completely alone in this room full of his colleagues. Even Arthur didn't understand the depth of his choices. It didn't matter how he explained himself. The bottom line was they would never understand why he did what he did and they weren't interested in sharing his pain.

"I won't consider the deal with the Syrians, but we have another opportunity in Spain that I'd like to have a look at. An old contact has resurfaced and — "

"Before we continue." Brian put a hand up. "Can I just confirm whether this is another one of your side projects? Or is this for the good of the company?"

"I consider all of our deals to be for the good of the company."

"What I mean is, will it make our shareholders happy?"

"You mean will it make you happy."

Brian shrugged.

"If you aren't happy with the direction I'm taking this company, Brian, I will not tie you down to anything."

"It was just a question."

Oliver could feel a headache arcing up the back of his skull. "This deal is for profit, yes."

The group spent the next hour working out the logistics of their next exporting venture. When they finished, everyone dispersed until only Oliver and Arthur remained.

"You look like you could use a stiff drink," Arthur said as he sat. "If only you drank. You sure you won't let me get you wasted? Just this once?"

Oliver smiled weakly. "It wouldn't help."

"You sure about that?"

Oliver shook his head, aggravating his headache. "I just can't understand where I missed it."

"It was an old boat. I was there."

"It's not that."

"Then what is it?"

"You wouldn't understand."

"Try me."

Oliver leaned back in his chair. "I fasted and prayed about it. I knew it could be dangerous, and I wanted to feel confident I was making the right choice. I really felt like God gave me the green light on it."

Arthur leaned an elbow on the table and let out a low whistle. "Don't tell those guys that. They'll eat you alive if they hear you're taking orders from a god."

"I know that."

"Look, it's hard for me to offer much reassurance since I don't share your faith, but I take it he doesn't shout in your ear?"

Oliver laughed. "No. It's closer to a quiet peace. It hasn't steered me wrong in the past."

"Never?"

"Well. I can't say I've never gotten it wrong. I'm only human, after all. But I was so confident this time."

Arthur shrugged. "Maybe that's your problem.

Doesn't the Bible say something about being humble? Maybe you were overly confident. Maybe it was pride." He leaned closer to his friend. "Or maybe it was just an old boat that wasn't able to make the journey. And your god had nothing to do with it."

"Maybe." Arthur was one of the few people he confided in at work, but he had never been able to explain God in a way that his friend could grab hold of in any meaningful way.

Oliver knew from personal experience that God could do the impossible. He just didn't do it this time. But ultimately Oliver wasn't the one who was going to have to pay the price for his failure, and he'd have to live knowing that others would suffer because of his mistake.

Chapter 4

MORGAN SAT on the lumpy couch with her legs crossed and Camilla's computer resting on her lap, still closed.

She hadn't had access to a computer in three years, during which time her handwriting skills had flourished. It had been cathartic during her imprisonment to write down her thoughts. Some days she'd write pages of notes as ideas poured out of her, but she'd immediately rip them up and throw them piece by piece in the trash, with some parts getting flushed down the toilet. She had learned a hard lesson about trust that saw her end up in prison, and she found it difficult not to think that everyone was out to get her.

Her thumb pushed the lock at the front of the computer, and she opened it slowly, taking several deep breaths while she waited for the machine to fire up. For something that used to act as another limb, she now felt trepidation at the thought of using this one.

The outdated Windows program appeared on the screen asking for a password.

A small laugh popped from her throat. Camilla had given her permission to use the computer but had failed to offer the password. Morgan was grateful, as it now forced her hand to reengage with her past.

Her fingers weren't as nimble across the keys as they used to be, but it wasn't long before the buoyancy of success fluttered in her stomach.

She took a moment to savor it before going into the back end of the system to fish out a couple of common bugs and weed out a close-to-harmless malware. Then she uninstalled all the unused programs, deleted duplicate files, and reconfigured the computer so it would function more efficiently.

It was still an underperforming system for her standards, and Camilla probably wouldn't notice the difference, but right now it was all she could offer her friend for her support.

As she breezed her way through the system, she considered the possibility of buying something more substantial for herself with the money she'd received from the government. Or if waitressing tips were as good as Camilla said, she might even save up enough extra for a quality computer. But she had to admit that would serve no purpose except to pour salt on the wound. No one would hire an ex-con who'd been imprisoned for hacking a banking system, no matter how innocent her record now proclaimed her to be.

Once she was satisfied with the state of the operating system, she got online incognito and opened a secure search engine, entering the name Ben Killian.

Her first stop was his LinkedIn profile, where she read through his credentials and portfolio. He'd done well during the years she was incarcerated. His hair was different, but he still had the dimples. His profile said he was engaged.

She kept searching and found a news article that listed him as one of the recent graduates of the specialized extended PhD program for computer science students.

They had both had the grades and talent required to apply, and they both submitted their applications at the same time, but because Morgan was at the top of her class, she was guaranteed a spot. Ben was not.

It was his idea to go to the bar and celebrate their expected inclusion into the program. They got drunk, and he kissed her. It had been so unexpected she almost didn't kiss him back, despite the fact that it had been what she was waiting for.

She touched her fingers to her lips and wondered now why he had done it. Was it an apology, knowing that he was about to be responsible for ruining her life?

She thought she had made peace with it, but seeing Ben living the life she should have had brought a seeping bitterness to the surface that she didn't know she had buried.

She pushed on the disembodied bruise by opening an employment website and searching for jobs she could have been applying for if she hadn't gone to prison.

Then she sat in a ball of gratified pain as she scrolled through the list.

When Camilla finally emerged from her bedroom at ten thirty, it was a welcome distraction from Morgan's current search — the less intrusive but still painful exploration of the best software programs available to date.

Morgan's eyes lifted from the screen, and she watched as her roommate stretched, scratching her fingernails on the top of the door frame and bending her mouth into a face-mangling yawn.

When Camilla's glassy gaze dropped to Morgan, she jumped. "I forgot you were here." She laughed. "Can you believe that?"

Morgan smiled. "I forgot I was here when I woke up too."

"At least you don't need permission to pee anymore."

Morgan refrained from informing Camilla that she'd never had to do that, but knew it wasn't her point. Camilla was an anomaly to Morgan, who tended toward the efficiency of a pragmatist and rarely blurted out the first thing that popped into her head, unlike her new roommate.

"Oh, I almost forgot." Camilla spun around and ran to her room.

Dropping to the floor, she reached under her bed and pulled out a small box, then came back to the living room and tossed it to Morgan. "A little 'welcome to the real world' present."

Morgan turned the wrapped box around in her hands. "You didn't have to do this. You've done more than enough already."

"Oh, don't worry. It's for my benefit as much as yours. Open it."

Morgan pulled off the wrapping and found that Camilla had bought her a phone. "You didn't have to do this."

"So you said, but I need to be able to call you. It's a cheap one, just a basic android with a prepaid, but it's a start."

Morgan dug her fingernail into the packaging and ripped it off as Camilla swished around the chair and flopped into it. "Now for your surprise."

"Wait. This isn't it?" she said, holding up the half-opened box.

"No way, are you kidding? I've got something much better."

"I wish you'd tell me," Morgan said, narrowing her eyes.

"All in due time. Just let me get some coffee into me, then I can show you."

It was two more hours before Camilla was ready to go, and it was the last time Morgan waited by the door, expecting to walk out any moment. At least she had her new phone to program.

When they finally stepped out onto the street, a warm breeze greeted them, settling Morgan's mood on the twenty-minute walk to the subway.

Camilla noticed the serene look on Morgan's face. "Freedom suits you."

"Yeah. Maybe it's not as scary as I thought."

"Hang on. Have you been scared?"

Morgan's honesty was unintended. "No, not like that. It's just taking some getting used to. But I am feeling better."

But when they descended below the city, the momentary relief was gone and Morgan was glad she wasn't alone. After living a life that had been ordered and predictable, Camilla's constant chatter kept her focused and gave her stability among the chaos of the pressing throng. It was going to take some time to get used to being free of her cage.

"This stop is us," Camilla said, fisting her hands in excitement as the train slowed.

"Can't I at least have a clue?"

"Hmm. A clue … a clue." Camila looked around the car for inspiration. "Fresh," she finally said.

"That's your clue?"

"It will make sense in a minute."

The train stopped, and they shoved out the door, Morgan trailing behind Camilla through the humid corridors until they climbed onto the busy streets of Manhattan.

"My friend Carlos is close by."

"He sells something fresh?"

Camilla giggled. "Something like that." They rounded the corner, and Camilla put a hand up to stop Morgan. "Here we are."

She flipped her hand over to showcase the sign for a hair salon.

Morgan's gaze defocused through the window, and she put a self-conscious hand to her head. "What's wrong with my hair?"

"Nothing is wrong with it *per se*. I just thought it could use a little *freshening* up. You're starting a brand-new life and there is nothing like a new hairdo to start over."

Morgan flipped up the ends of her hair to look at the tips. "I guess I could use a trim."

"Uh … yeah, a trim." She pushed Morgan through the door.

Inside was an elegant mixture of warehouse and chic made up of white-painted brick and gilded mirrors.

Morgan would have preferred the stifling subway over this place. It was less suffocating. "I don't think I can even afford to breathe the air in here," she whispered.

"It's on the house," Camilla whispered back, and before Morgan could argue, a short, stocky man with a shiny bald head came from the back and hurried toward them.

"Camilla. You're late." His annoyance conflicted with the laugh lines that were set deep into his face.

"You know me, Carlos." Camilla kissed his cheek. "Thank you so much for fitting us in."

"I had no choice." He turned his attention to Morgan. "She saved my life, you know."

Camilla waved him off. "You're so melodramatic. But it's true, in a non-death sort of way."

"Same thing," he said. "If I had lost my business, I would have died."

"Again with the drama." Camilla sighed.

"So." Carlos lifted Morgan's hair. "This is my canvas."

"Do whatever you think best," Camilla said.

"Hang on," Morgan said. "I thought I was just getting a trim."

Carlos glanced sideways at Camilla. "I thought you said she was on board."

"She is. She just needs a little coaxing. Listen, Morgan. I love you to pieces, but we can do so much better. You just have to trust me. And if you don't, that's fine. I'll just coerce you with threats."

"What kind of threats?"

She put a confidential hand to the side of her mouth. "You're really going to ask me that?"

"Are you saying you'd kick me out? You have every right to."

Camilla let out an exasperated breath. "Well, no. But let's pretend I would."

Morgan considered everything Camilla had already done her for her. "Fine. But I don't want anything too fancy. Natural is more my thing."

"How do you feel about short with a bit of color?" Carlos asked, leading her to a chair.

"Not too short. And no crazy colors."

Camilla spun the chair away from the mirror. "Okay, but you have to wait till the end to see."

Morgan gripped the arms of the chair as Carlos

leaned close to Camilla. "What's too short and how crazy is crazy?"

Camilla whispered back, "It's all relative."

Carlos pulled scissors from his belt and snipped the air. "I can work with that."

Morgan watched her hair pile up on the floor. "This feels short." Her fingernails dug into the vinyl seat cover.

"Not *too* short, trust me." Carlos said, continuing to flit around her head. "We're just taking the bulk out before the color, then we'll finish with style."

"I hope I don't regret this," Morgan mumbled.

"I haven't lost one yet."

Chapter 5

CARLOS SWITCHED off the hair dryer, and Camilla clapped while pressing her shoulders up to her ears. "It's perfect."

"Well? Can *I* see it?"

Carlos spun the chair to face the mirror, and Morgan coughed out a surprised chirp. It was exactly what she was afraid of, but she had to concede that Camilla was right. She looked great. "It's red."

"It suits you." Camilla said, standing behind her and resting a hand on each shoulder. "What do you think? Do you love it? I love it."

Morgan opened her mouth. She wanted to be mortified by the drastic change, but she wasn't. "I do, actually. Carlos, you've done a surprising job. Thank you."

Carlos lifted his eyebrows, creating a wave of furrows up his forehead. "That's not a compliment I hear often, but it's been a pleasure. And good luck to you. Come back anytime. No need to book an appointment. If you just need a trim, I'll fit you in."

. . .

Morgan was still touching her hair when they sank back into the subway to return home. A sultry breeze swept through the tunnel, brushing the back of her naked neck. It should have been invigorating, but instead, she was engulfed in weariness. Even though she loved her new hair, so much change in a short amount of time was overwhelming.

To the side of the corridor, a kid who looked to be about thirteen kicked the bottom of a vending machine, then slapped it hard on the side and the front. "Come on." His voice cracked in his frustration.

Camilla was busy talking about a new top she was thinking of buying when it went on sale, but Morgan stopped listening, instead focusing in the side of the kid's face. He was angry and frustrated for sure, but she saw pain there too. His bright-green sideways cap, wife-beater tank, and chunky boots suggested he wanted to be cool, but the grimace on his face belied his attempted attitude.

She tapped Camilla's elbow to stop her and turned to the side, heading for the teenager.

Morgan pulled out her phone. "You need a hand?" she asked, downloading an app.

The kid jutted out his chin. "No." Then he sucked in a cheek and a dirty grin appeared in place of the consternation. "Unless you wanna — "

Morgan put her hand up. "No. Just stop." She still had her eyes on her phone, waiting for the app to install. "I'm trying to help. This thing ate your money, yeah?"

He crossed his arms, and his eyes shifted to Camilla, who was watching in amusement. "You want a piece of this, b — "

"Hey." Morgan snapped her fingers at him. "Leave her out of this. You want your drink or not?"

"I don't need your charity," he said, leaning back onto the machine like he owned it.

"And I'm not giving you any." After the app downloaded, she lifted her phone over the panel on the vending machine that took payment. The app connected with the internal computer.

The kid stretched his neck, trying to get a look at her screen. "Wha'cha ya doin?"

"Decompiling the APK."

"Uh … why?"

Her eyes darted up to him, then back to her phone. "So I can extract the Java source."

Her finger repeatedly slid up the phone as she scrolled through the log.

"Wait. Are you *hacking* this thing?" He jerked a thumb over his shoulder.

"Yeah," she said, focused on her screen.

Camilla had tucked in behind her to watch. The kid soon followed so he could see, too.

"This is so cool," he said, shoving his hands into his armpits. "I didn't even know you could do that."

She found the "userwallets" table and added enough credit to buy him a drink, then pressed her phone against her chest to hide it. "So you've already paid for the drink, and it's taken your money?"

"Yeah."

She looked back at her phone. "Good." She hovered the phone over the pad on the vending machine. "Go ahead and press the button again."

He did so, and the drink dispensed. He pulled it out, accentuating his admiration with several swear words, then said, "Will you marry me?"

"No."

"Will you teach me how to hack vending machines then?"

"No."

"Will you let me kiss you?"

Morgan snorted. "Definitely not. Enjoy your drink."

Morgan walked away, and Camilla trotted after her.

"That was outstanding," Camilla said while they waited for their train. "Don't think the kid deserved it, though. He was kind of a troll."

"Maybe, but I saw something of myself in him. Lost and wanting to be tough to protect himself from the world. But only really pretending."

"Funny. I know that feeling, but I didn't see that."

"And you're supposed to be an excellent judge of character?"

"I am when I want to be. Punk kids in the subway don't always bring out the best in me. I guess I've seen too many. Experienced too many."

"It's helped my mood, anyway." She didn't mention that she was dreading stepping back into the working world the next day. Getting her head into a computer was a good distraction, but her stomach remained tight with worry about what was to follow.

Oliver walked along the sidewalk with his hands stuffed in his pockets. He had been on the phone all morning after a shipment that was due to leave the docks the next day got stuck on the thruway behind a ten-car pileup. He'd had to call in a favor to make sure it got loaded in time.

Then he had another guy try to hold him for ransom by demanding more money or he'd bail. He called the man's bluff, thanking him for the opportunity to cancel the deal so he could use another source that was cheaper. That got the guy back on board. But after dealing with the different crises, he needed some air.

He checked his watch and groaned. Time to head back.

Cutting through an alley as a shortcut to round the block, he stopped midstride when he heard a loud bang and a pained yell.

He jogged ahead and peeked around the corner. A kid with a bright-green hat was being hauled to his feet by a guy twice his size. The poor kid was no match for the man who looked like he worked out for a living.

When the man raised his fist, Oliver called out and raced toward the pair. "Hey!"

The man shoved the kid back into the garbage bins. "Stay out of this." He cocked his head to the side in warning.

"I can't do that. I don't know what he's done, but I will not let you bully him." He reached down to help the kid up.

"Oh-ho. Tough guy." The man shoved Oliver.

"You had better back off."

The guy took another step up to Oliver. "Make me."

Oliver was a few years older, but the two were close in size. He forced the guy's hand by dodging around him, knowing he'd make a move. When he did, Oliver used his momentum to spin his opponent around and send him sprawling across the alley.

After hoisting up the kid, who scrunched his green hat against his chest and didn't say a word, Oliver sent him on his way before the big guy was back on his feet and ready for a fight. But now that the kid was safe, Oliver was finished too. He backed up to leave the alley while monitoring his foe.

"Where do you think you're going?" The guy made a bull rush for Oliver, who dodged again, sweeping him away into a pile of garbage.

It was a fight Oliver was confident he would win, but regardless of his ability, he didn't like to fight if he could help it and was glad to find he wasn't followed onto the street after that.

On his way back to the office, Oliver savored the adrenaline rush. It had done him good. He'd been too stuck in his head. The only downside was his shoulder was aching again. He stretched it out but considered it a minor inconvenience for the relief of the other.

Chapter 6

MORGAN BLINKED AWAKE and squinted at the ceiling while she passed through the fuzziness of sleep. But something about the ceiling wasn't right. The sheet tangled in the crush of her fist as she struggled to make sense of the view above.

It took longer than the previous morning to remember where she was. The anxiety crippled her until her head cleared and yesterday's events renewed in her mind.

Her hand drifted to her head to pinch a chunk of hair. She rubbed it between her fingers.

A soft knock had her up on her elbows as Camilla poked her head in. "Oh, good. You're awake — Whoa, look at that hair. It's all over the place."

Morgan pressed a hand to her head. "Give me a break. I just woke up. What are you doing up so early?"

Camilla checked her phone. "It's almost eleven."

"Are you kidding?" Morgan kicked her feet over the side of the bed. "How did I sleep so long?"

"Guess you needed it. Come on. We've got to get moving. You have an orientation thing happening at work."

Morgan slid her hands down to her face and pressed her fingers into her eyes. "Right."

"And I've got another surprise for you," Camilla sang.

Morgan groaned and fell back onto her pillow.

"Wasn't my last surprise a success?" Camilla said as she came into the room and jumped on the end of the bed.

"I might be too exhausted for more surprises." Morgan ran a hand through her messy hair. "You going to give me a proper hint this time?"

"I can do better than that. I'll tell you all about him on our way in."

"*Him?*"

Camilla giggled and ran out of the room. "Hurry up," she called out. "We'll have to do something about that hair before we leave."

Camilla didn't say another word about the surprise while they were getting ready, and Morgan thought she'd get lucky and it would be forgotten.

But then they reached the subway, and Camilla poked her. "So, this *him* I mentioned."

"Oh, right. I was hoping I'd imagined it."

"No, no, no. This is a good thing. I've been so excited for you to meet him. He often eats at the restaurant, or sometimes he just does work there and has a drink, but I think he'll be there tonight."

"So he's a customer?"

"Yes. He owns a company in the city, and he's loaded. I think he might be from Europe somewhere originally. His accent isn't strong, but it's there."

"I take it he must be very good-looking if you're this excited about him?"

"Oh, yeah. He's like a better-looking version of Roger Federer."

"The tennis player?"

"Yeah."

"I thought Federer *was* pretty good-looking."

"Sure, but Oliver is even better-looking."

"Oliver." She said his name like it was a bad taste in her mouth.

"Yeah, Oliver Wright."

"Look, Camilla, I appreciate your care and concern for me. But I've just gotten out of prison. The last thing I need to add to my plate is the hots for some guy."

"Just wait till you *see* him."

"Hang on a minute. Why are you trying to palm him off on to me? If he's so amazing, why don't you go after him for yourself?"

"No way. Not even close to my type. I'd only be after him for his money and that's not my style, but you. I think you two would be perfect together."

"You know us both that well, do you?"

"You already know I'm an excellent judge of character, and the gift extends into matchmaking as well."

"You ever read the book Emma?"

"I've seen the movie. Does that count?"

"Yeah, that'll do. You remember what happened when Emma interfered in the love lives of her friends?"

"Yeah, but that's a movie. They have to make it dramatic. In real life I'm actually quite good at it."

"And how many lucky couples have you matched up in your life?"

"I knew you'd ask that."

"It's a reasonable question given the circumstances."

"Technically none, but on paper, I've done well with several. I always know which celebs are going to get together and which ones will break up."

"Celebrities."

"Yeah."

"Cami, you're killing me."

By the time they arrived at their stop, Camilla had begun giving Morgan a rundown of all the things she knew about Oliver, which wasn't much and mostly consisted of articles she'd read about him or his business.

But as they neared the restaurant, Camilla's prattling wasn't enough of a distraction anymore and Morgan's thoughts became consumed with dread about starting work.

When Camilla pointed out the restaurant ahead, Morgan's feet refused to go farther. "I can't do this."

Camilla pushed Morgan sideways to avoid colliding with other pedestrians and put a hand on her friend's shoulder, looking into her eyes as if she were checking for a concussion. "Hey, you're really stressed out."

"I'm sorry. I know you had to pull strings to get me a job here, but I don't think I can do it."

"But you have waitressing experience. It's like riding a bike. You'll slip back into the swing of things in no time."

"It's not that."

"Then what is it?"

"I don't know, but it's like a vice has closed around my body and I can't breathe. All I want to do is run home and hide. I'm so sorry."

She was hyperventilating, and her vision was shrinking. She'd never had a nervous breakdown before, but she was pretty sure that's what was happening.

Camilla took Morgan's hand and squeezed it. "Hey, listen." She forced Morgan to look her in the eye. "There is no pressure here. I can take you home if you want."

"Really?"

"Sure. It's no big deal."

Morgan's breathing slowed, and Camilla didn't speak again until she was confident her friend was in control of herself again.

"I can take you home, but I just want you to know that my uncle knows about your situation, and he's more than happy to have you. There are no expectations on you today, so if you wanted to try it, and it doesn't work, or if it turns out to be too much, I can show you a large comfortable closet where you can hide if necessary. Then, if you disappear, I'll know where to find you."

Morgan chuckled, appreciating her friend. "You have a solution for everything."

"Almost everything. But if you think you can take at least a baby step, tonight shouldn't be too busy, so I'll be able to cover for you if you fall apart. Although I don't believe you will. Just do as much as you can. I think it will be good for you to at least give it a try. If it doesn't work, we can figure something else out."

"What if I have a panic attack in the middle of the restaurant or something?"

"You won't. But like I said, I'll cover for you whatever happens. Just, at least come inside and meet my uncle Fred."

For someone who appeared shallow and giddy, Camilla was surprisingly compassionate, and Morgan felt bad about her sometimes sharp assessment of someone she called a friend.

"I don't know how I could have survived out here without you these past couple of days. You're the only friend I have in the world."

"Wow, you're unexpectedly blubbery. It doesn't suit you at all." She pinched Morgan's arm, teasing, then pulled her to the front of her uncle's restaurant.

"Welcome to *Gauge*, a trendy but casual fusion bar-restaurant in Upper Manhattan," Camilla rattled off her spiel like she were reading from a magazine.

"Fancy."

"Wait until you see the inside." She pressed her nose to the glass door and knocked, keeping her face planted until a figure emerged to let them in.

"We're going to have to clean that now," came an

excessively smooth voice that sounded like it had been whipped to just short of separating. "Face-prints don't go over well with our clientele. Why didn't you use your key?"

"'Cause I forgot it." Camilla fogged the glass with her breath.

"Then why didn't you go through the back like the rest of the employees?"

"Because I'm not like the rest of the employees, am I, Sal?"

"Don't remind me." The lock clicked. "Just because your uncle — "

"I was referring to my position as assistant general manager. I wanted to show Morgan — our new employee — the restaurant. Which I am entitled to do." She gave the door a hard shove to push past Sal, and Morgan quickly followed her inside.

"Sal, this is Morgan," Camilla said with the sweetness of a saint. "She's the new waitress." Out of the corner of her mouth, she added, "Sal's the host."

"Maître d'hôtel," he corrected, then looked down his straight nose at Morgan. His velvety voice dropped a notch. "I hear you've recently joined us from prison. What an extraordinary oversight."

Camilla tipped her head to the side. "It's actually none of your business."

"I beg to differ. It is my business to ensure the presentation of this establishment is impeccable. I'd like it to be noted that I do not agree with the hiring of a criminal into a well-respected restaurant with a flawless reputation."

"Noted, but she was pardoned, so your objection is irrelevant."

"She lived with hardened criminals for years. You can't tell me that didn't rub off."

"Oh, shut it, Sal. Where's Fred?"

Sal's lips pinched into nonexistence before he could bring himself to respond. "In his office."

"Thanks. That will be all."

He gave her a withering stare, then turned it on Morgan. "Don't expect Frédéric to offer the same courtesies to you as he does to his niece." He spun on his heel and went back to making sure everything was precisely as it needed to be for the evening's dining experience.

Camilla snickered. "I love doing that to him. He's such a snob. I have to take him down a notch every now and then."

Morgan looked around at the opulent surroundings. Round globes dangled from the ceiling, casting a soft glow over the white tablecloths. The spaces between the mirrors on the wall were decorated with flower mosaics that appeared to move in the low light. Then her eyes lifted to the inlaid marble ceiling. "This place is beautiful."

"I'm glad you like it. Sometimes I forget to notice. I've been here so long I take it for granted. Did I ever tell you I was sixteen when I started waitressing here? It was just after you moved."

"Really?"

"Yeah. Unusual for a place like this to have a sixteen-year-old serving, but my mom and I had the biggest fight, and I ran away from home. I think Uncle Fred felt sorry for me and wanted me to have a reason to stay. I'd often come in on my days off when I needed to get away from her and I'd peel potatoes in the back. We had a head chef named Louie back then and I think he felt sorry for me, too. He always fed me when I was here. But I really loved the hustle of the place. In the back, it's buzzing all night. So I did my job as best as I could and just kept working my way up."

"I take it you weren't the one who hired Sal?"

"No. My uncle does most of the hiring and firing, but Sal's actually brilliant at his job. He just takes himself too seriously, is all. Okay, that's enough reminiscing. I better introduce you to my uncle."

Camilla knocked on the half-open door of her uncle's office and then took Morgan's elbow, pulling her into the room. "Uncle Fred. This is Morgan. Morgan, this is Fred."

Fred stood and shook Morgan's small hand with his meaty one. Then he took a step backward and tucked his fists onto his hips, looking her up and down like he was inspecting a cow he was thinking of purchasing. He wasn't smiling. "So you're the ex-con?"

Camilla slapped his arm with the back of her hand. "I told you she was exonerated."

"Cami says you have extensive waitressing experience?"

Morgan shifted uncomfortably. "I waitressed to put myself through college, yes."

"She didn't tell me you were a college graduate."

"Uh. Sort of. I was in the middle of my masters and looking to get into a PhD program."

"I see. And what was it you went to prison for?"

"Uncle Fred," Camilla said between gritted teeth.

He pushed harder. "What was it?"

"Computer fraud," Morgan answered.

"And do you expect to go back to college?"

"It's been three years, and it's very competitive. I can't see how that would work."

Fred glanced at his computer and nodded. "Okay. We've got some spare uniforms in the back. Find one that fits and we'll order some more for you once I'm satisfied. Tonight will be a trial, but as long as you keep your nose clean, we won't have any trouble. I don't mind giving someone a go, especially if Cami gives you the all clear."

"Yes, sir. Thank you."

"All right. Off you go," he said to Camilla, before he sat back at his desk.

Camilla led her out of the room and into another before speaking. "I'm sorry about that. I expected him to be more polite."

"That's okay. It's what I'd expect. Innocent until proven guilty is a fairy-tale."

Camilla laughed. "You're so pessimistic. We'll have to do something about that. But looking on the bright side, I take it you aren't freaking out anymore?"

"No, I'm okay at the moment."

"Good," Camilla said, lifting a box off a shelf. "Then we better get you dressed."

. . .

Morgan cringed at her reflection in the mirror. She had rolled the bottom of the too-long pants and now pulled at the snug-fitting top. She had to keep her shoulders rolled forward so she didn't pop a button. The only other choice was a shirt four sizes too big. Morgan would have gone for it, but Camilla wouldn't let her.

She gave up trying to think of a better solution and went to the staff room where Fred found her and gave her another appraisal.

"Hmm. I guess it will have to do for tonight. Here," he said, handing her several sheets of paper. "Fill this out and get it back to me by the end of the night. Where's Camilla disappeared to?"

"She said she was checking on the dining room."

Fred nodded with a grunt and left.

Morgan stared at the paperwork. She had always known her social security number by heart, but couldn't remember it while she looked at the empty squares.

Camilla swung around the corner. "He's here," she said breathlessly.

"Who?" Morgan asked as she squinted at the space for the address of her last employer. "I did work at the prison. Does that count?" she said to herself.

"Leave that for now. We've got plenty of time for that later. But now I want you to come see."

"Come see what?" Morgan said, stabbing at the paper with the blunt side of the pen.

Camilla pouted. "Not what. Who."

Chapter 7

CAMILLA BOLTED BEHIND the bar and squealed under her breath. Morgan didn't know such a thing was possible.

"Right over there, see?" Camilla said, looking back at the door they had just emerged from. Morgan turned, and Camilla smacked her arm. "Not that way. Behind me."

"But you were looking over there."

"Yeah, I can't look at him. It would be too obvious."

"I can't begin to fathom how you became assistant manager acting like this." Morgan scowled, then slid her gaze to the side, past her friend's head, and spotted a quiet table near the window. A man sat facing away from them, his dark hair tied at the back of his head.

Morgan leaned her weight onto her heel and crossed her arms. "No way."

"What? Are you kidding?" She turned now to gawk at him freely. "Look at his shoulders. Not just any man can fill out a suit like that."

"Yeah, but he's got a man bun. I don't do man buns."

"You're so racist."

Morgan looked at her friend sideways. "That's not racism."

"Well, what's that other word then. From that other book they made into a movie." She snapped her fingers. "Prejudice."

"A little pride, maybe, but I'd say it's closer to simple good taste."

"Morgan, I hate to remind you, but you've been behind bars for the past three years. Your idea of taste may differ from the general public. Just wait till you see his face."

"No, thanks. I'll pass." She turned to go back and stare at her paperwork again, but Camilla grabbed her arm.

"You don't have a choice. He's seated at one of your tables for the evening."

"Are you serious?"

"Yep, off you go. Quick, before Sal notices one of his favorite patrons is being spurned."

"Oliver is his favorite?"

"They're all his favorites. Stop stalling."

Morgan breathed deeply, unsure if she was more resistant because she was about to step back into the working world, or because she would be serving the man who Camilla had arranged for her to marry. She preferred to get the whole ordeal over with, for both reasons. Then she could get on with her life, and she and Camilla could move on to other topics.

She gripped the hem of her shirt and tugged, then set off to serve Man Bun.

———————

Oliver read the latest report from his contact in Libya, who had confirmed that four villagers had been murdered in the night and a fifth villager likely had been abducted. It was an event Oliver could have prevented. He slammed his hand on the table, then realized someone was standing beside him. His head jerked around to the newcomer and he blinked a double take. He hadn't seen this server before.

"Sorry to interrupt, sir. But are you ready to order? Is there anything I can get for you this evening?" Morgan's eyes darted to the computer, and he folded it shut in reflex, leaving his hand covering the lid.

"I've lost my appetite, unfortunately, so I'll just have mineral water."

"Yes, sir." Her mouth squeezed into a tight smile. Or at least, that's what she was aiming for. She collected the superfluous tableware and turned away to hide her snarl.

Oliver's hand twitched on top of the laptop as he watched her go. He'd never had a waitress give him a dirty look before, and it was a surprising distraction that pleased him, although he couldn't understand why. Maybe it was because he was tired of being flirted with, or perhaps it was the irony of how it fit with his day. Why not add to the list of people he had disappointed this week.

"So, how'd it go?" Camilla asked, biting her lip. "He's gorgeous, right?"

"He's got a nice face, but he's a jerk."

"What? What happened? What'd he say?"

"He smacked his hand on the table when I interrupted him, then when he looked at me, he said he'd lost his appetite."

"Really? That doesn't sound like him. He's always been super polite to me. Good tipper too."

Morgan shrugged. "Maybe he doesn't like redheads."

"Everybody likes redheads."

"I thought that was blondes. Anyway. The funniest part was when he slammed his laptop shut to stop me from seeing what he was doing. What he doesn't know is that I could just hack it and have a look if I really wanted to."

"You can do that?"

"Sure. Not that I would."

"Maybe it was top secret stuff that no one was allowed to see."

"If it's confidential, then he shouldn't be working on it here in the first place."

"He's probably just had a bad day."

"Why are you defending him?"

"I'm not. I'm just saying that's not like him."

"I guess I must just be lucky." She shrugged like it didn't bother her. "I better get his drink before he blows a fuse."

. . .

Morgan waited for the order at the bar, drumming her fingers on the counter. "Not a great first customer," she growled to the bartender as she retrieved the drink. She carried it flawlessly to the table, balanced neatly in the center of the tray. Her irritation had given her a renewed aptitude for her job. Maybe she should thank him for the favor.

He was looking at his computer again, so she kept herself angled away from the screen and lifted the drink to set it on the table so as not to disturb him.

He reached up and put his hand on the glass to take it from her, touching her fingers. "Thank you."

The smile he offered was so genuine, it startled Morgan, and she jerked her hand away, nearly spilling the drink. "Sorry," she mumbled and slunk off.

Camilla scooted up next to her. "See, I told you."

"Don't ever make me serve him again."

"But he just apologized."

"You were listening?"

"I made an excuse to be close enough to hear, yes. I wanted to see what was going on. I don't know why he was rude in the first place, but that was definitely an apology."

"I didn't hear the word sorry except from me."

"But that's what he meant."

"Do you read that much into all the things *I* say?"

"Of course. I'm superb at reading people."

Morgan's eyes lifted in an exaggerated arch. "Uh-huh."

"For example, you said *uh-huh*, but you don't actually believe me, am I right?"

"Did you discern that from the eye-roll or the grunt?"

"Listen, you're just wound up because it's your first day. Tomorrow will be better."

"As long as you leave me alone about Oliver Wright."

"You're breaking my heart." She bumped Morgan's shoulder with her own. "I know what you could do."

"No."

"Hack into his company and find out more about him."

"That's illegal."

"You're telling me you never used your computer skills for evil?" Camilla smiled devilishly.

"That's not the point. I just got out of prison for that. I don't intend to go back in anytime soon."

"You're no fun at all."

"I'm glad you're beginning to get me."

"No, that's not you."

"This is becoming painful, and I've got work to do, unless you want me to go hide in the closet … "

"All right. I'll leave it alone."

The small flick of a smile flashed across Oliver's face as he recalled the redhead's response to his kindness. It was a shame she hadn't succeeded in spilling the drink onto his computer and shorting it out so he could have a moment of reprieve from his trouble. It would have made his day a whole lot better.

Instead, he was now staring at the email he was attempting to compose. The blank page mocked him as he took a sip of water. He had to come up with another way to help them, but he was getting so much pressure from his board to focus on the profit margin, it was hard to process. Even with Arthur on his side he found himself railroaded.

The only people who understood what he was trying to achieve were on the other side of the world and in grave danger, and he could do nothing about it.

The redhead walked past and served a table close to his. He watched her for a minute, but her presence was making it uncomfortably hard to focus. He wasn't going to get any more work done, so he finished his water, tucked a fifty under the glass, and left.

———

Morgan had seen Oliver staring at his screen with his fingers pressed into his forehead as she served the tables around him. When he left, he looked like he was carrying the weight of the world, and she hated to admit that Camilla may have been right. When she considered her own uphill battle with peoples' perceptions of her, perhaps she should have given him the benefit of the doubt.

. . .

The rest of the night went well and Fred was happy with her performance, but when she left for the night, Camilla hanging off her arm, her mood spiraled into a hole.

"You did well tonight," Camilla said when they got home. "Why do you look so down?"

"It's nothing."

"Are you still upset about Oliver?"

"No, it's not that. He actually left me a fifty-dollar tip."

"I told you he was sorry."

"Maybe. But it's nothing to do with him. I just worked so hard to get into college only to now have a future set out before me as a waitress."

"Waitressing isn't so bad."

"No, of course it isn't. It's a really great job with great tips, just like you promised. But I always had my heart set on computers. That's what I'm best at."

"Well, don't give up yet. You don't know what's just around the corner. You've got your whole life ahead of you."

"We're like a modern-day Odd Couple, you and I. We have completely different views on life."

"Opposites do attract."

Chapter 8

MORGAN PUT the kettle on the stove. It was the first night she and Camilla had off together all week. Camilla had begged to go out, but Morgan needed the respite. She'd made it through the week with no more anxiety attacks, but she was looking forward to a night in, insisting Camilla go ahead. But in the end, they both stayed at home and ate what Camilla called a "Seniors" dinner of frozen pizza before five o'clock.

Morgan ripped the packaging off the chamomile tea bag and dropped it in the mug while she waited for the water to boil. She'd never been much of a tea drinker, but she was finding it hard to relax without something to wind down with.

After several minutes staring at the kettle, she left it to boil and leaned on the doorway facing into the living room to watch a few minutes of the reality TV program Camilla was catching up on.

One of the contestants, Brody, a good-looking athletic guy in his twenties, was talking to Lucy, a forty-year-old mother of two, or so the text at the bottom of the screen read. Brody was explaining why he had betrayed Lucy during one of the games.

"What an idiot," Morgan said. "Just because it's all part of the game, doesn't make it okay. Does he really think she's going to forgive him?"

"Sure."

Morgan crossed her arms and watched as Brody explained to Lucy that he'd probably do it again if it would help him win. His hand was resting on her knee and Morgan wished Lucy would stab it with the pencil she was holding.

Morgan grunted her disgust as the video changed to show Brody now in deep conversation with another guy on the show. They were the same age, but this other guy was skinny and had a high-pitched nasally voice. Brody was saying the same things he'd said to Lucy.

"So, has he gone and stabbed everyone in the back?"

Camilla twisted around in her seat. "You know, for someone not interested in this show, you sure are interested."

"It's like slowing down to look at a car accident."

The screen changed again, and Brody was apologizing to another contestant.

Morgan shook her head. "I don't get it. Don't they vote each other off?"

"That's why he's apologizing."

The kettle screamed, and Morgan dashed back to turn it off. "And he really thinks apologizing is going to make it all okay?" she called out from the kitchen. "This stuff makes me crazy."

"Then you'll be pleased to know they're doing an eviction tonight."

"Oh, good." Morgan said, bringing her hot mug back into the living room and taking a place on the couch. "I might watch that part. I wouldn't mind seeing Brody kicked out."

"Don't hold your breath."

"How could that possibly disappoint me?"

"'Cause I don't think they'll actually vote him off. He's too charismatic. Everyone loves him."

"No, they don't. They hate him. He just admitted to being a traitor and saying he'd do it again." Without a second thought she took a sip of tea too fast and burned her tongue. She sucked in air to cool it off before saying, "Just 'cause he says it nicely doesn't make people okay with it."

"You'd be surprised."

"That's ridiculous."

"You want to bet?"

Morgan laughed. "Are you serious?"

"Sure. Why not?"

"Well, who do you think they'll vote off?"

"I think it will be that girl Kate."

"Which one is she?"

"The quiet one."

Morgan shook her head. "That doesn't even make any sense. Wouldn't the quiet one be less of a threat?"

"Logic has nothing to do with this stuff. Everyone on here acts according to their emotions with no thought to what is right or good."

"Fine, what are we betting?"

"If you win, I will do the dishes all of next week."

Morgan stared wide-eyed. "*All* the dishes?"

"All of them."

"I'm beginning to like this betting thing."

"That's just 'cause you think you can't lose."

"I can't. But just in case I do, what's the other half of the bet?"

Camilla pressed a finger into her bottom lip. "Hmm." Then her eyes lit up. "If you lose, you have to hack into Oliver's business."

Morgan was stunned into silence. She had to blink several times before she could speak. "No way."

"Why is everything 'no way' with you when it comes to Oliver?"

"It has nothing to do with Oliver and everything to do with the law. Besides, I thought we were done with him."

"Nah, I was just giving you a breather. I still think he's perfect for you."

"This bet is not even. There is a big difference between washing dishes and breaking into a network."

"What's the big deal? I just want to prove to you he's everything I said he was. Read a few emails from employees or something to see what they have to say about him. That's it."

"Do you know how much trouble I could get into if I got caught?"

"You think you'd get caught?"

Morgan knew she wouldn't. "I can't believe I'm even contemplating this."

"If you won't get caught, then what difference does

it make? You can't lose. Now hurry up, the ad break is almost over. What do you say?"

Morgan looked at the TV. She really wanted to see Camilla actually do the dishes for once. "Okay, it's a deal."

The program went back through the remaining six contestants before getting around to the vote.

Morgan tipped her head back onto the couch. "This is taking forever. How long are they going to drag this thing out?" she whined. "Dishes need to be washed."

Camilla slapped her. "Shut up. They're about to announce it."

Morgan chewed on her fingernail as they montaged each contestant one more time before finally showing the evictee. Kate's devastated face appeared on the screen and almost completely mirrored the look on Morgan's face.

"That's impossible. This wasn't a rerun, was it? Did you already know?"

Camilla didn't even try to hide the wicked laugh. "It did run last night, but I didn't watch, I swear. I had no more idea than you did except I obviously know people better than you do."

"But he *told* everyone he'd do it again." Morgan slapped her hands onto her head. "It doesn't make any sense."

"You do know that reality TV has nothing to do with actual reality, right?"

"Doesn't it? Because now I'm terrified that this

represents the general public. That is a very scary thought."

Camilla lifted her laptop and set it on Morgan's lap. "Off you go. Find some dirt."

"I can't believe this. What is wrong with people?" she said to herself as she started working off her bet.

"Right now, I don't care. I just want to know more about Oliver." Camilla curled up next to her friend so she could get a good view but had no idea what she was looking at.

"So you have no qualms about breaking into his private life?" Morgan asked as her fingers tapped an uneven pattern across the keys.

"It's not his private life. It's his business. And it's not like you're reading his diary."

"I could, if it were on the network."

"Seriously?"

"You just got a little too excited at that. I have to draw the line somewhere." Her fingers paused for a second. "For such an impressive company, their IT department sure could use a brush-up."

"You're in?"

"Not yet, but it looks like all I have to do now is create a buffer underflow."

"Ah, of course. That's what I was thinking. And how will you do that?"

"Just get the pointer index to decrement to a position before the buffer." She squinted at the screen.

"Okay, well, let me know when that pointer starts decrementing."

"Any minute now … and … voilá!"

"We're in?"

"We're in."

"I can't believe it was that easy."

"It wasn't *that* easy. I mean, you have to find the weakness, and getting access to the pointer index wasn't that simple."

"You sure make it look easy."

"That's 'cause I'm that good." She didn't bother suppressing her grin. "And here is the email server. What are we looking for?"

"Can you do, like, a filtered search on that thing?"

"Sure."

"Seriously? This is like online shopping."

"That makes me feel so much better about what we're doing," Morgan said dryly.

"Oh, come on. Like you haven't done this a hundred times before."

"It's a gray area. But mostly I've operated in the white."

"So I've corrupted you?"

"Sure, let's go with that scenario. What do you want me to search?"

"Oli, Oliver, hot stuff? But filter out any emails from him obviously." She waved her hand toward the screen. "We don't care what he thinks of himself."

"Don't we?"

"No. I want to hear what his employees have to say."

Morgan typed, squinted, and typed some more. "I'm going to have to narrow this down further ... Let's see ... Oh, this looks promising."

As they read through the emails, Morgan's face

reddened. "Do people not realize that Oliver could easily look at these emails? IT has access to all of this stuff."

"Is that normal?"

"Yeah. All these emails are the property of the business. It's common knowledge that if the boss wants to see what you've been looking at online, he or she can."

"Yikes. Well, Oli is certainly well-liked by all. Look at this, she's calling him Kingy. We've seen that a few places. Try searching for that."

Morgan leaned back. "Don't you think we've done enough? I'm feeling squeamish."

"Last one. I promise."

Morgan stretched her neck. "Fine."

She did the search and a line of code flashed across the bottom of the list of emails and then was gone.

"Hang on." Her fingers sped across the keys, digging into the source code, and she found it again. She bit her thumb.

"What is it?"

"You ever heard of the dark web?"

"Is that like where people go on the Internet if they don't want to be seen? Like black market stuff?"

"Something like that. Sometimes you can find it on business networks. It's a privacy thing for those who have access to the network setup. They can create a sort of *dark web* on the server where only a select few have access."

"It can't be that secret if you just found it."

Morgan shook her head. "I only found it by accident and only because I'm in the data access layer. Usually, that's the only way to even know it's there. Searching for it can take days or more, and you don't even know if it's really there or not unless, or until, you happen upon it. Mostly, it's not worth the bother."

"Why not?"

"Because most businesses don't use it. If you're looking to commit a crime, your time is better spent focusing on what's in front of your face, not searching for something that may not even be there."

"And we've just happened upon it?"

"Yeah, if I hadn't been paying attention, I would have missed it. There's something about that last search."

"So Oliver has set up an undercover web thingy?"

"Not necessarily."

"Well, open it up. It's perfect. Exactly what we're looking for."

Morgan frowned. "I shouldn't. This is kind of like the diary scenario. It's hidden on purpose."

"Come on, just a quick look. Just for Kingy."

Morgan tapped her finger on the couch cushion, then moved her hand back to the keyboard. "Just for Kingy, then I'm out."

"Deal." Camilla bounced up and tucked her feet under her butt, keeping a close eye on the screen.

Morgan brought up the corresponding emails and together they skimmed through them.

"Something's not right here," Morgan said, moving to another email.

"Oliver can read these, right?"

"Well, these are different. Whoever set this up only

gives access to those he wants to, and judging by these emails, I'd say Oliver does *not* have access."

She kept reading until she reached a line that talked about removing *Kingy* from the picture and a plan that had been put in motion to do it.

Camilla said, "Oh man, it looks like they're trying to get rid of him."

"I thought he owned the company."

"Maybe they're organizing a hostile takeover?"

Morgan's stomached tightened as she moved onto a string of quick emails. "No. This isn't good. I think this is really, really bad."

I wish we could meet.

It's not safe.

And emails are?

These are. Everything is in place for tomorrow night.

Promise me it's untraceable.

You need me to spell it out for you again? He won't drop dead until he's well clear of Gauge, and if they discover it's not from natural causes, there is no way it will lead back to its source. They'll be looking elsewhere. We are in the clear.

What about the bartender?

> I've already arranged for his disposal after the job is done.

> I don't understand why we have to kill him.

> I've explained that to you. We have too much riding on this, don't tell me you're trying to back out now.

> Of course not. I just want to make sure we've accounted for everything.

Morgan checked the date on the emails. It was from the previous day.

Camilla grabbed Morgan's wrist. "They're going to kill him?"

Morgan jumped up from the couch and pressed her fingers to her chin, trying to think. "Is there a number for Oliver? Do you have his number?"

"If only."

"What about the restaurant? Um. I'll go down there now. You get your uncle on the phone."

"What am I going to tell him?"

"Just ask him if Oliver's there. Tell him not to let him drink anything, or eat anything for that matter, and keep him in the back in the office. I'll get down there and explain everything."

Chapter 9

MORGAN FLAGGED DOWN A TAXI, but in her panic forgot the name of the restaurant or where it was located. She smacked her forehead several times before she remembered it was mentioned in the email.

"Gauge. Take me to Gauge. It's an emergency."

It was drizzling, and the blend of muted streetlights and the swish of the windshield wipers heightened Morgan's anxiety. The drive was interminable, with each swipe of the wipers a possible moment Oliver took the poison.

Scenarios plagued her mind of walking in the door just as he walked out, and she'd be too late. It felt like a bad dream where she needed to run, but her legs wouldn't cooperate.

She pecked her fingernail against the door until she noticed the driver eyeballing her in the rearview mirror, so she tucked her hands under her legs.

Just before they reached the restaurant, it occurred to her that if she made it on time, she would need to explain how she knew what she knew. Could she simply tell Oliver that she hacked into his system and expect that saving his life was enough to stop him from pressing charges? She couldn't face prison again, but the only other option was to stand by and watch a man die.

The taxi pulled up to the curb before she could find a suitable answer, so she grabbed a wad of cash from her bag and chucked it at the driver as he slowed.

The cab was still rolling when she jumped out and raced into the calm and cool atmosphere of the restaurant.

"Morgan." Sal was startled at her appearance, but not enough to slow him down. He stepped in front of her with his hand raised, and she skidded to a halt. His face was a serene and reassuring mask to any patrons who may have looked their way, but his words were sharp. "You shouldn't come in this way. Just because you're friends with Camilla doesn't give you the right to — "

She didn't have time to explain her presence to the maître d'. Instead, she used the moment of pause to scan the room, only half listening to his reprimand.

Oliver wasn't at his usual table, but the restaurant was full tonight. Her eyes passed by the bar and she confirmed the presence of a new bartender, but she still hadn't spotted Oliver. Fred may have already removed him to the back. Or maybe he didn't come tonight. But then she finally located him at a corner booth.

"Sorry, Sal, just passing through." She dodged around the host, who swiped at her but missed.

Morgan saw a waitress she'd worked with, named

Kate, headed in Oliver's direction with a drink. Morgan hurried to intercept, not realizing that Sal was right behind her.

She weaved around tables and made it to Oliver at the same time as Kate, whom she then bumped from behind as the drink was being set down. It spilled down Oliver's front.

"Oh, I am so sorry," Kate said, then spun around to pin her eyes on Morgan.

"Morgan? What are you doing?"

Sal was on the other side of her and echoed her name, but his tone was not a questioning one.

"I, uh." Morgan focused on Oliver, who was dabbing at his shirt and waiting for an explanation. There was no way she was giving it with Sal and Kate there.

"Sorry I'm late, Oliver," she said, sliding into the booth. A hot flush rushed up her face. "I was in too big a hurry and now look what I've done."

Oliver stopped wiping his shirt and watched her.

"M-my apologies, sir," Sal sputtered. "We'll get you a fresh drink. On the house, of course." He nodded to Kate, and she bolted for the bar. "Morgan, I'd like to have a word."

"It's not her fault," Oliver said. "I told her it was urgent. She was rushing because of me. No harm done." He put his napkin on the table and folded his hands, smiling.

Sal glared at Morgan. "Very good, sir. Are you sure there is nothing else we can do to assist? I'd be happy to offer a complimentary dinner. Or perhaps we could find a change of clothes if you'd like?"

"You keep extra clothes here that are my size?"

"Well, uh. No. But perhaps we should."

"Only if you expect this to happen again."

"No, sir. This was a onetime occurrence that I can assure you will never happen again."

"Great. Then I'll be fine."

"Very good, sir. I hope you enjoy your evening." Sal delivered this line mechanically in the absence of anything more suitable to say.

"I'm sure I will. Thank you."

Kate returned with another drink, setting it carefully on the table while watching Morgan, who was staring at the glass. "Will there be anything else?"

Oliver looked at Morgan and slid his hand across the table to get her attention. "Would you like a drink?"

Morgan's head shot up. "No," she said too quickly.

Oliver smiled. "You came all this way, I think you should order a drink."

Morgan was flustered and looked up at Kate. "Coke. I'll have a Coke."

"You don't have to drink it," Oliver said when the waitress left. "But it looks rather conspicuous if you come in here and order nothing. Especially since I apparently invited you here." He reached for his glass.

Morgan forced a smile onto her face and spoke without moving her lips. "Don't dink dat."

Oliver didn't lift the glass but spun it slowly on the table. "Today started out very ordinary, but it has just become much more interesting."

"Interesting is not the right word for it." Her eyes traveled around the room.

"Then I really do hope you're going to give me a better explanation. I am sitting here soaking wet after all."

Morgan put her elbow on the table and rested her mouth on her hand so it covered her words. "I think someone is trying to kill you."

Oliver nodded. "Is that so? And who might that be?"

"I'm not sure yet, but the bartender is new."

Oliver looked around the room, his eyes sweeping past the bar long enough to see the man behind the bar. He was wiping down the counter and had his eyes on their table, but he glanced away when he was discovered.

"Since I have no way to confirm or deny your claim, I'm going to play it safe and believe you."

He lifted the glass to his lips and Morgan's eyes widened, but he didn't drink anything. Instead, he had positioned his hand to cover the side of the glass. "Tell me when he looks away."

Morgan turned her head casually, taking Oliver's previous lead. She watched the bar with her peripheral vision. "Now."

Oliver slipped his glass to the side and poured some onto the floor. "If Sal could see me now."

Morgan was surprised he was being humorous at a time like this. "I'm sure he'd prefer that over your death."

Kate returned with her drink. Morgan thanked her but didn't touch it.

Oliver nudged his own glass with his fingers. "True. A customer dropping dead at one of his tables would be worse for business."

"No. You wouldn't die at the table. It's not supposed to kill you till later." He looked at her and lifted an eyebrow. "Or so I'm told," she quickly added.

"By who?"

"No one. It's a figure of speech."

He lifted the glass and pretended to drink again. "Tell me when."

"Now."

He poured the rest of it on the floor. "You haven't touched yours."

"Can you blame me?"

"You aren't very good at covert. Shall we go before we're discovered?" He set the empty glass on the table.

She hadn't even thought about what she would do next. "Uh. Okay."

Perhaps he was satisfied just being saved, and she could go home knowing she'd done a good deed without having to worry about revealing her actions and getting into trouble.

He stood, and she followed him to the door.

Sal stepped forward. "I'm sorry to see you leaving so soon. I hope you enjoyed your time with us tonight. And again, I am extremely sorry for any inconvenience we have caused."

"I had a lovely evening. Thank you." Oliver took Morgan's hand when he saw the host eyeballing her.

Morgan stiffened, and Sal's lips did a quick pucker of indignation at the intimate gesture. "We look forward to serving you into the future. Morgan, may I have a word before you go?"

She looked at Oliver, unsure why she was asking for his permission. She was the one responsible for saving his life, but he seemed to know what to do next, whereas she was at a loss.

He nodded, and she stepped aside to speak with Sal. "Yes?"

"I hope you realize that fraternizing with customers is frowned upon at this establishment."

"I'm not fraternizing. We're just friends."

"Make sure it stays that way."

Oliver interrupted. "I'm sorry, but we really must be going."

"Very well, sir. Have a lovely evening."

Oliver nodded and opened the door for Morgan. Once outside, he handed in his valet ticket and folded his arms across his wet chest.

Morgan looked down the road. "So, I guess I'll see you later?"

"What did Sal want?"

"He wanted to make sure we weren't dating."

"Good to know he has his priorities straight."

She took a step sideways. "All right, well. I should get back. My roommate will want to know how this all went."

"Your roommate knows about this?"

"Uh, well." Morgan tripped as she moved sideways again. "She kind of … She knows something's wrong."

A BMW pulled up to the curb.

"Get in the car," Oliver said, heading for the driver's side.

"No thanks, I'll take the subway."

He stood at the door. "No, you're coming with me."

She scoffed and shuffled closer to him but kept the car as a barrier between them. She lowered her voice. "I just saved your life. I think that's plenty."

"You need to get in the car." He didn't wait for her to answer this time, just got in and pulled the door shut. When she didn't oblige, he put down the passenger-side window.

She leaned over. "I'm not getting in your car."

"You afraid I'm trying to get an actual date with you? Don't worry, you're not my type. Now, get in, unless you want your life to be in danger."

The valet was watching the exchange. With that and the new fear that Oliver was right, she got in the car.

"So you have a roommate?" he asked her as he pulled away from the curb.

"Yes, she knew I was coming to see you, and she'll be concerned if I don't return."

"You need to call her. You're not going home tonight."

Morgan pulled her bottom lip into her mouth when a new thought ran through her head. She knew nothing about Oliver. What if the people who were trying to kill him were doing it because he was a terrible person?

"I think you need to let me out. Now."

"I'm not going to do that."

She flinched, and he realized he would to have to be softer with her if he was going to keep her on his side.

He needed more information, and right now, she was the only one who had it.

"Wait a second." He turned the corner and pulled the car over. "I won't hurt you. You allegedly saved my life, and I'm just trying to return the favor."

"How? By scaring me?"

"Listen, Morgan — "

"How do you know my name?"

"Both Sal and the waitress said it."

"Oh. Right."

"How long do you think it's going to be before the people trying to kill me realize what happened? Before they know I'm not dead?"

"I don't know. They said it would take a while for the poison to work."

"Right." Oliver pinched the bridge of his nose. "And how long after that do you think it's going to take before they realize you're involved? That you're the one who interfered with their plan?"

"How would they know that?"

"It doesn't take a genius. You put on a pretty impressive performance that most people in the restaurant would have noted. Especially the bartender who you allege is involved."

"Why do you keep using that word?"

"What word?"

"Allege."

"Because I'm not convinced."

"But it's true."

"I believe you think it is, but I never take one person's word. Well, not a stranger anyway. I'm going to need to verify it, but in the meantime, in case it is true, you need to call your roommate and tell her to get out of the house. It's only a matter of time before they search for you there."

"What if she has nowhere to go?"

"The street is better than death."

Morgan's mouth dropped open and a small squeak escaped her throat.

Oliver sighed. "Is that really the case?"

"Well ... no ... but ... I just ... I can't believe this is happening." She rubbed her hands down her face. "I was just trying to help."

"I'm sorry for the trouble this is creating for you, although I appreciate it and I'm very grateful. But unfortunately, there are consequences to your actions that you obviously didn't take into consideration, and I feel it's my responsibility to make sure you don't pay a higher price than you already have."

"Why are *you* so calm about all of this? Shouldn't you be the one freaking out instead of me?"

"It's not the first time my life has been threatened."

"Really?"

"Would you please call your friend? It will put my mind at ease."

He pulled back onto the street while she made her call.

"Morgan. I'm so glad you called. Did you make it in time? Uncle Fred wouldn't pick up, and when I called the restaurant, Sal refused to put me through. He said I shouldn't be tying up the business line for personal reasons, and then he hung up on me. Can you believe it?"

Morgan allowed a small pause to make sure Camilla had finished her monologue. "That sounds like Sal. But it's okay, 'cause I made it in time. Oliver's safe, but now I've made a mess of everything."

"Not everything," Oliver said.

"Wait, is that Oliver I can hear?"

"Yeah, I'm with him now in his car, but I'm so sorry Camilla. I've put us both in danger. You need to pack some things and go stay with your mom for a couple of days until I get this sorted." The line was silent. "Camilla, are you there?"

"You want me to stay with my mom? I'd rather sleep on the street."

"Do you have some other place to go?"

"I'll figure something out. Where are you staying?"

"I don't know yet."

"Okay, well, stay safe."

"You too."

"And Morgan?"

"Yeah?"

"I couldn't have planned it better if I'd tried."

"What?"

"You and Oliver."

"You can't be serious," Morgan hissed as she pressed the phone hard against her ear and turned away, worried Oliver could hear.

"I'm just saying."

"Go pack."

"I'm going. Keep in touch, okay?"

After Morgan hung up, Oliver made a call. "Hey, Rog, can you do me a favor and change my security to level three? And you can expect a call from Peter Black. Oh, and I've got a shirt with a substance on it that will need to be analyzed."

After he hung up, Morgan said, "So ... are you a secret agent or something?"

"No, why?"

"You're getting people to analyze a substance and changing security to level three. Not to mention your life has been at risk before. Sounds like secret agent stuff."

"It's a long story."

"Um. So, Camilla is finding a place to stay, but what about me? I can't afford to live in a hotel until this is over."

"You're coming to my apartment."

"What? No."

"Don't worry. You'll have your own space, and I promise not to hit on you."

Morgan scoffed. "Like I'm worried about that."

"No? Then what's the problem?"

She couldn't think of anything that made sense. "Is it safe?"

"Security level three, remember? I'll send someone over to your place later to collect whatever you need. You can trust me."

"I'm not good at trust," she said, looking out the window beside her.

"Then perhaps it's best that you don't have any other option right now."

Chapter 10

OLIVER TURNED into the dark underground parking garage of the high-rise building he lived in. Out of the corner of his eye, he saw her stiffen.

"You okay?"

She audibly swallowed. "Fine."

Morgan forced herself out of the car and followed Oliver toward the elevator. The shadowy corners and echoing of their steps made it hard to trust this man she knew nothing about, but the light that appeared as the elevator doors opened eased her tension, and she stepped in ahead of Oliver, staying as far from him as possible. He noticed and smiled, keeping his thoughts to himself.

Her eyes were glued to the floor numbers as they climbed higher and higher and she wondered if she was imagining the sway.

When the elevator stopped, her stomach lifted, and she clenched her teeth before following Oliver into a hall with plush grey carpet. A crystal vase with fresh flowers sat on a long glass table that separated two doors. A man with dark hair haloing a bald spot stood near it with his hands clasped behind his back.

"I didn't know you had company," the man said.

"Part of the change in security. Roger, this is Morgan. She saved my life tonight. I think."

The man bowed marginally. "My thanks are in order then."

Morgan shrugged. "I didn't do much."

Roger's eyes rested on her for a moment longer before shifting to Oliver. "Is there anything else you'll be needing?"

Oliver unbuttoned his shirt and gave it to Roger. "This is the shirt I need analyzed."

"Anything in particular we are looking for?"

Oliver turned to Morgan for an answer, but she was looking away. "Poison of some type, I presume. Peter Black will likely be here by tomorrow. But I will need to arrange for someone to pick up Morgan's things."

"Urgently?"

"Tomorrow morning should be fine." He looked at Morgan again to get her approval, but she had her eyes firmly planted on the floor in front of her.

After Roger left, Oliver opened the door that was closest to him. "This is where you'll be staying."

Morgan followed him in, and because he couldn't see her, she didn't hide her surprise.

The room had a large desk against the wall carrying several monitors and a keyboard. A small open-plan kitchen filled the right side while a hall led down to the left.

A sitting area faced a large window looking over the city. Morgan was immediately drawn to it. "That's amazing. I've never seen a view like it."

"It is spectacular. Down the hall is a bedroom and bathroom, and at the end, that door leads through to where I live. It locks from both sides. So if you still don't trust me … "

"This isn't where you live?" She turned to him and put a hand up to cover her face. "Sorry, but could you put a shirt on? I'm just — it's distracting."

He laughed. "Yeah, sorry. Wait here." He disappeared down the hall through the door he had mentioned.

Morgan let out a deep breath while she looked around the room. The kitchen was bigger than her apartment.

"This is my office away from the office, as well as the guest quarters when I need it," Oliver said when he returned, buttoning up a fresh shirt.

Guest quarters, Morgan mouthed as she walked over to the computer.

"You can use that if you want. It's connected to the internet. You just turn it on with this button here." He walked over and pointed to the tower under the desk.

"I do know how to use a computer."

"Of course you do."

"What about a password?"

"No password."

"That's stupid." She sniffed, running a finger across the edge of the desk.

He smiled. "It will, however, scan your face and when it doesn't recognize you, it will send me an alert and I can give you access. Or I'll have you arrested. Depending on my mood."

She blanched but covered it. "Cute."

"I thought so." Oliver looked at his watch. "Would you like a drink?"

"No, I'm fine."

"Before I leave you to settle in, I've got a few questions, if you don't mind?"

"Yeah, sure." She walked over to the window to hide her trepidation. She wasn't ready for questions, but probably never would be.

"How do you know about the assassination attempt?"

"I, um … I overheard some people talking."

"What people?"

"I don't know."

"Let me guess. It was dark."

Her mind was racing, grasping for a suitable response. "I don't know much."

"Just random details like how long the poison takes to work?" She didn't speak. "If you don't tell me, I'm going to draw my own conclusions."

That sounded better to Morgan than telling the truth. "Why don't you tell me what you think, and I'll tell you if you're right?"

"Okay. We can play it that way. I believe you were involved in the planning of this evening's event."

She spun around. "What?"

He was sitting on the couch with his arms stretched across the back and his ankle resting on his knee like this was an ordinary conversation he could be having with anyone.

"Maybe you had a boyfriend or a family member who brought you into it. Then you got cold feet. Couldn't go through with it. So you had to warn me."

"I had nothing to do with this." She didn't think there was a worse explanation than the truth, but he'd found one.

"How else would you know so much?"

"There are other ways."

"Such as?"

She scrunched up her face. "I'd rather not say."

"No, I'm sorry, but that's not acceptable. Unless you can convince me otherwise, I'm going to stick with my theory. And that's what I'll tell the police." He had no intention of calling the police, but she needed a nudge.

"Okay. Wait. I'll tell you … but you have to promise me something."

A muscle in his cheek flexed as he considered her proposal. "Promise you what?"

"That you won't press charges, and you won't tell anyone."

"That's quite a lot to ask."

"I did save your life."

"So now you're blackmailing me?"

Her mouth opened and closed like a fish out of water.

"Look, Morgan. I have no intention of doing either

of those things if I don't have to, but you're going to have to come clean before I can make any promises like that."

She covered her face with her hands and groaned, then dropped them in her lap. "Okay. I guess that will have to do." She took a deep breath. "I hacked into your business."

He didn't respond straight away, and she cringed at the expected response. "That is not what I was expecting."

"And?"

"What?"

"Are you going to press charges?"

"Did you do anything illegal?"

"You mean, besides the hack?"

"Yeah. Did you steal any data or anything?"

"No, nothing like that."

"As long as you've done no damage to my business, then I won't press charges."

"And you won't tell anyone?"

"Why can't I tell anyone?"

She pressed her fingers into her forehead. "This is such a bad day."

Oliver shook his head. This girl who had tripped across his life was not like anyone he'd met before. "I'd like to present the argument that it's been a worse day for me. So, you going to tell me?"

"I was just released from prison." Her fingers slid down her face, covering her mouth as if to hide her confession.

"Prison."

"For computer fraud."

He stood and combed his fingers through his hair. "So, this is what you do? You're a hacker?"

"No, I — I was at school for computer science, but I was framed for the crime. In the end, I was acquitted, but not before I had spent three years in prison. But it doesn't matter because it's painted me with that brush. If anyone finds out about this, they won't overlook my three years in prison."

"But you were framed. And it's no one's business."

"Maybe officially, but you can't keep that stuff hidden. They'd find out somehow. Just please don't tell anyone."

"Okay." He threw his hands out to the side. "I guess I can give you that assurance. So, when did you get out?"

"Last week."

His eyebrows shot up. "That recently? And here you are getting yourself into more trouble that you didn't cause. So you hacked into my computer system — even though you're not a hacker, which I will come back to — and then what? How does my business fit into all of this?"

"I found some emails."

Oliver let out a slow breath. "I see." He walked to the window. "So there is a chance, then, that this is all a prank? I mean, anyone who's smart enough to plan an assassination wouldn't write emails about it when I have access."

"They weren't on that part of the server."

He turned. "There's another part to the server?"

"A partition was created to make a private server on your network and whoever created that partition gives access to only those that he or she wants to."

"But you found it."

"Yeah."

"And how hard was that?"

"Close to impossible. I only found it by accident because of the way I was looking, and I'm very good. If I hadn't been paying attention, you'd be dead."

"Presumably. So can you tell who was writing these emails?"

"No. There were no names."

"What about the computers they came from?"

"No. There is nothing that could pinpoint a person. Not even your name was in there. It was all in code."

"That you could read?"

"Sort of."

"So how do you know they were talking about me?"

"They called you Kingy. That's you, right?"

Oliver put his hands on his hips and shook his head. "That started last year. I was on a trip to New Zealand and I went on a fishing charter. There was an incident with a kingfish. I never lived it down."

"That could be good, then. So it would have to be someone who knows that."

He shook his head again. "It's common knowledge. You can't keep that stuff hidden for long." He laughed. "Of all the things," he said to himself. "So what did these emails say exactly?"

"It would be better if I just showed you."

"By all means." He motioned to his computer.

Morgan sat down at the desk and set to work. "If you could get me in, it would be faster."

She slid sideways so Oliver could have access to the computer, but he crossed his arms and didn't move.

"I want to see you in action. Show me how you got in before." Half his face lifted in a grin.

Morgan flexed her fingers. "If you say so." She started typing. "You might want to have a look at your computer security. It's not up to scratch, by the way."

"Thanks for the heads-up."

He watched her work. It looked impressive, although he didn't quite know what she was doing. "Okay. So, going back to your imprisonment. I'm curious to know how you were acquitted. Did someone else confess?"

"No. Fresh evidence proved I couldn't have done it."

"But you spent three years knowing you didn't do it. Do you know who did?"

"It was my roommate."

"The one you're living with now?"

"No. When I was at college. He broke into a banking system and framed me for it in case he got caught."

"He."

"Yeah, why?"

"You were in love with him?"

"What? No, we were roommates, that's all."

"You didn't want more?"

"What does that have to do with anything?"

"It just seems odd that he could do that and get away with it, that's all. So he framed you on purpose."

"Yeah."

"Sounds like this old roommate of yours was better at framing than hacking."

Morgan snorted. "I've never thought of it that way before. But that's the thing that gets me the most. If it *had* been me, I wouldn't have gotten caught. My lawyer didn't think that was an appropriate argument to prove my innocence."

"Did your lawyer believe you were innocent?"

"He said it didn't make any difference. But of course it did to me. In the end, I'm pretty sure Camilla was the only one who believed me. She's the reason I'm out now. She convinced me to get a new lawyer and look for more evidence. At first I resisted. I'd accepted my fate, and I couldn't afford a lawyer. Camilla went looking though. She found someone who was interested in taking my case."

"Thank goodness for Camilla. If it wasn't for her getting you out of prison, I'd be dead."

She turned and looked at him. "That is a very interesting point."

"You ever think you'll go back to school?"

Morgan pressed her fingers into her forehead. "No."

"You've been asked that before?"

"Yeah."

"With your skills I doubt you'd need the degree to get a good job."

"Maybe, but the trouble is, I've lost my confidence."

"You seem pretty confident to me."

"That's not what I mean. Businesses want to see the degree before they see your skills. What am I supposed to say when they ask why I don't have a degree? 'Sorry, I was in prison, but don't worry, I was acquitted.' I don't think that would go over well."

Oliver leaned toward the screen when he realized she'd gotten access. It was disconcerting.

Morgan brought up the emails and moved so he could read them.

When he finished, his head dropped. "These emails are all internal?"

"Yes. I thought it might be worth sorting through to see if there were any outgoing ones. We might be able to connect someone that way."

He covered his mouth with his hand in thought, then stood and went to the kitchen. "Water?" he asked after filling up one cup.

"Yeah, okay."

He brought the drinks over and sat down. "So there are those at my company who are planning my demise."

"I'm sorry. Does anyone spring to mind?"

"There are plenty who'd like to have me out of the way, but to kill me to do it?" He shook his head. "I don't know who would go to those lengths. If you wouldn't mind having a look tomorrow for an outside connection, I'd appreciate it."

"Yeah, sure. I guess it's in my best interest as well, if I ever want to get out of here."

Oliver smiled sadly.

"Hey." She put a hand over his. "I know what it feels like to be betrayed by someone you trust."

He nodded. "I'm sorry that you're stuck here with me, but I'm glad you are."

She shrugged. "At least I'm not afraid of you anymore."

"I guess that's something."

Chapter 11

THE GLOW from the screen was the only light in the room when Morgan sat down at the computer the next morning. She had slept surprisingly well in the safety of Oliver's apartment despite the circumstances. But she woke early to the idea of having an assignment that involved computers. It was the place she felt most in control. And right now, control was the thing she needed most.

After she read through a list of numbers, trying to decide if they were relevant, a soft knock came from the door between apartments and she hurried to open it.

Oliver was dressed in pajama bottoms and a tee-shirt, holding two cups of coffee. One mug had a picture of Lionel Richie and read: *Hello ... is it tea you're looking for?* The other was plain blue.

"Morning," he said, handing her the blue one.

"How'd you know I'd be up?" she asked, inhaling the aroma from the cup her hands were wrapped around.

"I saw how energized you were working on the computer last night and I thought maybe you were as interested in getting started as I was. I hope it didn't keep you from getting some sleep."

"No, I slept fine. Hey, you don't have milk or cream by any chance?"

"In the fridge. There's sugar in the cupboard too."

While she went to adjust her coffee, he went to the computer. "How long have you been at this?"

"Only about an hour."

"Find anything interesting?"

"Oh yeah," she said, returning to the desk. "Turns out they deleted the emails overnight."

Oliver sipped his coffee. "I should have expected it, especially since they thought the job was done. So we've lost everything?"

"Of course not. I'm not an amateur, you know. I made copies of everything last night. And" — she sat down and brought up a document with notes, scrolling down to a highlighted portion — "does this company have a connection to you in any way? An email was sent to someone over there about a month ago. It was in the trash but hadn't yet been permanently deleted."

"Potters is a tech company I've been working with on and off for the last five years. They've recently had a breakthrough with battery technology. We've been discussing how that technology can be used to help in third world situations. I can't believe they're involved." Oliver set his coffee on the desk and stretched out his shoulder.

"The email is ambiguous and there was no reply

from what I could find, so a lot will depend on who it ended up with — You hurt your shoulder?"

"Old injury. Is it possible to get a name?"

"Name?"

"The individual's name where the email was sent."

"Oh, uh." She bit her nail. "Technically."

"Which means?"

"I can't get one from your system, but I'm confident I would get it on Potters' end. But … "

"You'd have to hack their system. Like you did mine."

"Yes. I had a peek already. They're way more advanced than you. It would likely take me all day. Possibly longer."

"But you could do it?"

"I think so. You want me to give it a try?"

"Having you search my company is one thing, but giving you permission to break into someone else's is another."

"I don't technically need your permission. I can pretend I didn't ask you if it would make you feel better."

"You know, for someone who was so adamant about being innocent against the allegation of hacking, you sure don't seem to have a big problem doing it."

"I was arrested for stealing other people's money. I don't do that. But we are talking about your life and that's different."

"So you're like a vigilante?"

"And you're not?"

"I'd like to think I'm not."

She folded her hands in her lap. "You're telling me you've never done the wrong thing for the right reasons?"

Oliver thought of the work he had done in the Middle East with Peter Black. "This is different."

"Why?"

"Because Potters hasn't done anything wrong."

"Someone at Potters may have."

"And what injustice were you putting right when you broke into my company?"

Morgan's face reddened. "You're changing the subject."

"No. It's the same subject. You didn't know my life was in danger until after you had a look around."

She knew he wouldn't let it drop, but that didn't make it any easier to come clean. "I lost a bet."

"So a real life-and-death scenario. And what would you have gotten if you'd won?"

"Camilla would have done the dishes for an entire week."

Oliver smirked. "Okay. That does sound like a worthy bet."

"Thank you. And just so you know. I only made the bet because I didn't think I could lose."

"So what exactly was it you were looking for?"

Morgan's attention flew back to the screen. "Can we just get back to Potters? If you want me to hack them, I should start now."

Oliver looked out the window at the brightening sky. "Let's just wait for now. I've got a friend coming. I'd like to bring him up to speed before we decide."

"What do we do until then?"

"Stay put. If you want to put together a list of the things you'd like picked up from your apartment, we can get that done."

"Yeah, about that. I think I'd rather go myself. I can go with whoever it is you were intending to send, but I don't want a stranger poking around in my underwear drawer."

"Fair enough. I think that would be okay."

Oliver went back to his place to get ready for the day and saw he had a missed a call from Arthur. He called him back.

"Hey, Arthur, sorry I missed your call. I hope it's not more bad news."

"Oliver … Hey … No, nothing like that. I was just checking in to see how you were doing."

"This early? Truthfully, not well."

"Not feeling well? Or … "

"Physically I'm fine, but I've discovered that someone might be trying to kill me." The line was quiet. "Arthur?"

"Yeah, I'm here. Sorry. I just … You think someone's trying to kill you? Why would anyone want to kill you?"

"I don't know."

"How did you find out?"

"It's a long story. You haven't heard anything? Even if it seems a small thing, it might help solve the mystery."

"Why would I have heard anything?"

"Because it's coming from inside Wright and Lavigne."

"You can't be serious. How do you know?"

"I've got a source."

"Wait. Someone from Wright and Lavigne?"

"No. An outside source."

"Are you sure you can trust this person? You haven't gone paranoid on me, have you? How can you be sure they don't have ulterior motives? What if they're making the whole thing up to manipulate you?"

"I'm looking into the specifics of the threat, but I trust her."

"I think you should tell me who she is so I can look into her background."

"It doesn't matter who she is. Just keep your ears open, okay?"

"Oliver."

"Arthur, I'm not going to tell you."

"You don't trust me."

"It's got nothing to do with trust. I don't want her to be involved more than she has to be."

"Fine. I'll see if I can find out anything on my end. But you're safe now? You've taken precautions, I take it?"

"We both know this isn't the first time I've had to do this."

"But those other times were not like this. Not assassination attempts on American soil. Could it be connected to overseas? How much does this source of yours know?"

"We don't know much yet. I'm still trying to gather more intel. All I know is the threat is real."

"Okay, let me know if there is anything else I can do."

"Thanks." His phone beeped in his ear. "I've gotta go, I've got another call coming through." He swapped over to the other call. "This is Oliver."

"Oli, it's me. I'm downstairs.

"That was quick."

"You said it was serious. I caught the first flight."

"Great, get Rog to bring you up. You've already been cleared."

Oliver opened his door and waited for his friend to arrive. While he was waiting, Morgan's door opened, and she stepped into the hall. "Oh, I was just about to come find you. I'm ready to go get my stuff whenever."

"Good. My friend, Peter Black, is on his way up. He's helped me with security in the past, so I've asked for his assistance."

"Your security guy's last name is *Black*?"

"Yeah, great name to have in this job."

"I went to a dentist once whose name was Steven King."

"Yikes."

"Yeah. Really nice guy though."

"I suppose Stephen King the author could be a nice guy too."

"True." Morgan nodded. Then they both turned as the elevator opened and an attractive man in his fifties stepped into the hall. He had a short beard and a strong face with the weathered look of a man who'd spent a lot of days in the sun. He smiled warmly when he saw Morgan

"Hello there." His voice was deep with a raspy edge. "I take it you're Morgan?" He took a step closer and held out a hand.

"Mr. Black."

"Please, call me Peter." He shook her hand with a strong grip before he turned to Oliver. "It's been a long time."

"Too long," Oliver said, reaching out to embrace his friend.

"So what's first?"

"Morgan needs to collect some things from her apartment. I thought we could go there now and I'll give you all the details on the way."

"I'm ready when you are."

Morgan listened to the two men reminisce on the drive. It was obvious they had a fondness for each other that was close to family, but they were efficient and careful in their movements when they arrived at her apartment.

Despite Peter's casual manner, there was a controlled power that she could sense just below the surface. Even with the possibility of a threat, she felt safe with these two men who knew what they were doing. Although, Oliver surprised her with his skill at reading Peter's movements, and his assistance in keeping her safe, especially since it was his life mostly at risk, not hers.

Peter unlocked her door and entered first, while Oliver watched their backs. She was apprehensive to enter herself, afraid it would be ransacked, but everything looked to be in its place.

Morgan grimaced when she found that Camilla had left the dishes in the sink when she left. Knowing they were there would haunt her.

"I'll just be a minute," she called out while she filled the sink.

"What are you doing?" Oliver said when he found her.

"Sorry, it will only take a minute."

"Come on," he said, pulling her away. "You get your things. Let me do this."

"You don't have to."

"No wonder you were so willing to make that bet with your roommate." He plunged his hands into the soapy water. "Do you know what the cockroaches would be like if these sat here for several days?"

"That's exactly what I was thinking. And thank you."

She watched him for a second before collecting her things.

The drive home was the same as the way over, with Peter and Oliver talking nonstop. Sometimes discussing business and sometimes telling stories.

When there was a slight pause in the conversation, Morgan took advantage. "How do you two know each other?"

Peter responded first. "I ran a private security firm that specialized in overseas work. When Oli had some

... things ... that he needed help while in the Middle East, he hired my team. We ended up working together on that project for, what, three years?"

"Yeah, had to be close to that. You taught me a lot in that time. Saved my life too."

"More than once by my count."

Oliver's phone dinged, and he checked the message. "And it looks like you may have the chance to add to the tally. It's the report on my shirt. I won't try to pronounce the scientific name of the poison, but that's definitely what it was. And it was in a concentrated dose that would have killed me."

Morgan sagged in her seat. "When you mentioned it could be a hoax, I was really hoping it was."

Peter turned the car into the underground parking. "Now we just need to find out why and who."

"About that," Oliver said. "Morgan's a bit of a computer nerd — "

"Hey."

Oliver turned in his seat. "Well, you are, aren't you?"

She made a face. "I wasn't talking about the nerd part." She mouthed the words *you promised*.

"Don't worry." He looked back at Peter. "She's found a connection through my business into another one. She has the ability to hack into the other business and maybe find a name, but ... "

Peter parked the car and ran a hand over his mouth. "You never struggled to operate in the grey zone when we were overseas."

"Is that so?" Morgan interrupted. "Vigilanteism at its finest."

"That's different and you know it. I've got a relationship with Potters, and I'd rather not do anything to jeopardize that. I also don't feel comfortable asking Morgan to put herself in that position."

"Hey, I offered."

Oliver breathed out a long sigh. "But I don't make these decisions lightly and I don't want to ignore the obvious."

"The Higher Power," Peter said.

"Right."

"Do you have any connections that you can be confident are not involved in the plot?"

"Raquel Suvo is the CEO. I don't think she'd have any reason to get rid of me. She's powerful enough in her own right. She doesn't need me out of her way for any reason."

"There's your way in."

"But I also don't want to accuse one of her employees of attempted murder when I don't have all the facts."

"I'm sure you'll think of something."

Chapter 12

"OLIVER, it's so good to hear from you," Raquel said in her usual confident tone that gave the impression she was the one in control but also someone you could rely on. "I was just given an update this week on our project. It sounds like everything is coming together brilliantly."

"Yes, your team is highly skilled, and I must say, very creative."

"And I've been just as impressed with what Wright and Lavigne have brought to the table. I must admit, when you first brought me your proposal, I was skeptical about how a company such as yours would operate outside their usual boundaries. I've been pleasantly surprised."

"I'm glad to hear that we are both benefiting from the project."

"Yes, I look forward to discussing future opportunities with you. But enough of the pleasantries and small talk. I assume this isn't a social call? What is it I can do for you?"

"I don't want to take up too much of your time. But I have a small favor to ask."

"I'm intrigued. Oliver Wright asking for a favor. From what I hear, you're usually the one handing them out."

"I'm not sure if you mean that as a compliment or not."

She laughed. "Oh, it's a compliment. I could warn you of the dangers of being known as someone who offers easy favors, but you don't strike me as a man who allows himself to be taken advantage of. Just generous in nature."

"I certainly hope so. On both accounts."

"Don't keep me in suspense. What is it I can do for you?"

"I've got someone new working with me. Highly skilled when it comes to computers. Recently, she discovered a breach in our system."

"Oh my. You've been hacked."

"Something like that."

"What's the damage?"

"Thankfully, she found it in time. But it was a big threat."

"So she stopped it?"

"Yes."

"Interesting. Sounds like you don't need my help then. You are in excellent hands. It's not often hackers are intercepted *in medias res*."

"Well, the problem is, there is still a threat that we haven't been able to identify and while she was looking into it, she found a link to Potters."

The line was quiet for a moment. "You're saying one of my staff is involved?"

"Honestly, I can't say for sure. Not without looking into it further."

"You do realize we vet our employees probably more thoroughly than the FBI?" There was a pause and then her voice went steely. "Are you going to give me a name?"

"I don't have one yet. That's the problem."

"Then what is it you need from me?"

"Permission to enter your system so she can find the name."

"Pardon me?"

"She believes she can get the information we need from your end."

"I don't suppose you will give me the time to check her out?"

"We don't have the time, but I do trust her with my life. Literally."

"Literally? You never fail to surprise. Unfortunately, when it comes to the security of my business, your word is not enough. No offense."

"None taken."

"But I'll tell you what I can do. I think there is a solution. A way we can both benefit and not put my organization at risk."

"That's what I was hoping for."

"I'll give you permission to attempt to gather the information you need, but we will record every keystroke. And entry into our system is completely up to the skills of this computer genius you think you have on your hands. I'd like to know if there are any chinks in our armor that we are unaware of. I expect her to act discreetly and to be aware of what she is accessing. If she downloads anything or goes anywhere unnecessarily, we will know."

"Deal."

"Just be warned, if she's as good as you say she is, we might poach her."

"You can try," Oliver said with a smile. If Morgan got a job with Potters after all this, that would be the perfect gift for her after the trouble she'd gone through to help him.

"I look forward to seeing how she performs. Oh, and Oliver." The pitch of her voice lifted into a lighter tone. "We're giving a small party, and by small, I mean extravagant, to celebrate. It's a prelaunch for the battery. Have you been invited?"

"Yes, I believe I have."

"Wonderful. I hope to see you there. And if your computer savant turns out to be all you expect, bring her along too. I'd be delighted to meet her."

"I'm sure you would."

Oliver found Morgan still at the computer. "What are you looking for now?"

"Just mining the information we already have, hoping for another lead." She stretched and yawned, then rested her head on her hand.

"Anything?"

"No. Nothing that will help."

"That's okay, because Raquel has given us the all clear, so you're good to go on that one. She's sending through something to download so they can record your keystrokes and make sure you don't have any devious intentions. I told her I trusted you, but those were her requirements."

Morgan barked out a laugh. "Oliver, you're probably the only one on the planet who expects people to be true to their word. I'm not surprised she made that stipulation."

"I'm glad it won't bother you."

"Oh, it will bother me. I don't like being watched. But I don't really have a choice, do I?"

"No."

"Anyway, this is good news. I'll get started on that today." She cracked her knuckles.

"You really love this stuff."

"I really do and maybe I shouldn't."

"Why not?"

"This is your life we're talking about."

"No need to feel bad. I'm glad you enjoy it. If you hated it, I would probably be dead."

"We keep adding to that list, don't we?"

"What list?"

"Ways you'd be dead if things had been different. I just don't want you to think that I'm not taking it seriously."

"You don't have to worry about that. I'm very grateful for everything that you're doing for me. Especially when it shouldn't involve you."

"Besides the danger to my life aspect, it's certainly better than waitressing."

"Good." Oliver looked at his watch. "Okay, well, I'm going out." He turned for the door.

"Wait, what? I thought we were supposed to stay put."

"I'll have Peter with me and the chance is pretty low that they'll make a move in the open."

"Can I come? Or no. I should stay here and get started."

He shrugged. "You can come if you want."

"Where ya going?"

"Church."

She snorted, then dropped the smile when she saw that he looked genuine. "You're serious?"

"Yeah."

"Oh."

"Something wrong?" He lifted an eyebrow in fake concern. He hadn't been surprised by her response.

"No. Of course not. I just didn't take you for a churchy guy."

"Well, I am. But it's actually been over a month since I've been there, with all the travel I've been doing. I miss those guys."

"How's Peter feel about it?"

"You worried about him?"

"Just curious."

"He's churchy too."

"Really? So when you and Peter mentioned a *Higher Power*, you literally meant God."

"Yeah. Who did you think we meant?"

"I thought you were talking in code. That explains a lot."

"Like what?"

"Like why you were hesitant for me to hack into Potters. That is a serious conscience you have there."

"I try. So you want to come?"

"Man, the last time I was in church I think I was eight."

"Didn't like it?"

She shrugged. "It was okay."

"So … you coming or not?"

"No, I think I'll get started on this. Right now, I think it's a tad more important."

Oliver didn't think so, but he certainly wasn't going to push. "Suit yourself."

Oliver stepped through the double doors of the church with Peter bringing up the rear. He breathed in the smell that reminded him of a library. Peter moved up beside him and scanned the room.

"I think we're pretty safe in here," Oliver said in response to Peter's careful examination.

"It's my job, Oliver. Let me do my job. Once I'm satisfied, I'll relax."

Oliver did his own scan, but for different reasons. The large open space was filling with people. A teenage boy whose name he couldn't remember was carrying around a little girl on his shoulders with two more trailing behind him, impatiently waiting their turn. Two women were in deep conversation in the front row. One had tattoos up her neck and the other wore a knitted sweater and slacks, with tassels on her shoes. They both looked like they had tears in their eyes.

This was a church you couldn't hide in. It was a church full of people who were there because they wanted to be and because they wanted a place to belong. With about seventy people each Sunday, every newcomer was noticed and with no stage lighting, you couldn't sneak in once the service started. Someone always saw you and made it their mission to at least say hello. Everyone who walked through the doors was invited to their own place in the menagerie whether they wanted one or not. It wasn't for everyone and it wasn't perfect, but Oliver loved it.

While the church itself was started seven years ago, the hall was new to them. They'd moved in at the beginning of the year and still had plastic chairs set up in rows. At the time, the heating wasn't working and blankets were used to keep everyone warm. Oliver had made it several weeks in a row back then, a record for him, and he had already mentioned to the pastor that they should skip the heating come winter and stick with the blankets.

Oliver finished his appraisal and his searching gaze settled on a tall, broad man in his early forties who was up front shredding on his guitar. The sound on the amplifier was turned low so the twangs from the metal strings sang out louder than the notes. The man's head was bowed and swung back and forth as he jammed. He finished with a flourish and looked up, spotting Oliver.

His face beamed as he leaned his guitar against a chair. Then he pointed at Oliver as he traveled down the thin aisle like a train about to derail.

"Oli! I didn't know you were coming." He grabbed him in a bear hug with several big pats on the back. "Man, it's good to see you. What's been happening?"

"Isaac, it's good to be back."

Pastor Isaac was a loud preacher who said what he thought and didn't cower in the face of conflict. But he was also quick to apologize if necessary and also quick to forgive. He never pretended to be anything other than what he was, which put some people off, but he was wise enough to make up for his shortcomings by creating a great team around him with different strengths. They gave the church a solid ground to stand on and made room for God to do what he wanted.

"Oliver!" came another yell from behind him before he could respond to Isaac.

Oliver and Peter turned in unison and spotted a petite woman with long straight hair striding their way. She had a little girl on her hip who got squashed between the two of them when she gave Oliver a kiss on the cheek. The two-year-old grabbed fiercely to her mother and eyeballed Oliver with surprising malice. Oliver smiled at the girl, who hid her face in her mother's shoulder.

"Lauren, I got your text about bringing some food to share, but I completely forgot."

"How could you? You know how much I look forward to eating your brownies." Lauren winked.

"Oh, you mean the ones I brought in last time on

my grandmother's antique foil pan that's been passed down from generation to generation?"

"Yeah, what was her name again?"

"Betty Crocker."

"Right. What an amazing woman she must have been."

"The best."

Isaac piped in. "I don't know how you two can joke about food. It is a very serious matter. Do you know what would happen to this place if we ran out of muffins?"

Lauren snorted. "Yeah, like that would ever happen. If there is one thing you could never accuse this church of, it's starving people on a Sunday morning." Her attention shifted to Peter. "Hi, I'm Lauren." She hefted her daughter higher on her hip and shoved out her hand for Peter to take.

"Sorry, guys. This is my friend Peter. He's visiting from out of state. Peter, this is Isaac, Lauren, and Layla."

"Nice to meet you," Peter said. "Oliver's told me very good things about you two. And she," — he dropped his gaze to Layla — "is about as cute as they come."

Layla flailed back into her mother's shoulder after realizing she was being talked about. Lauren tugged on a pigtail as a crashing clang echoed through the hall. Peter reached into his jacket and moved to block Oliver. They all looked over to see a tray of cookies had been pulled onto the floor by a stray toddler whose mother was frantically gathering the spill. Someone nearby scooped up the startled child while two more joined the mother on the floor to help clean up the mess. Lauren passed Layla off to Isaac and went to help. "Nice to meet you, Peter," she said before heading to get a broom.

Oliver frowned while he watched her go. He'd gotten to know both Isaac and Lauren well over the years and found Lauren to be brutally honest about her shortcomings and insecurities. He knew from her own admission that she struggled to let others take the load.

A church split the year before brought Isaac pretty low and Lauren was left carrying a lot of the responsibility. They came through it stronger than before, but he still worried about his friends.

"I better go do the rounds." Isaac said, slapping Oliver on the arm. "Nice to meet you Peter." He bounced Layla as he moved on to a family that had just walked in.

Before Oliver and Peter could advance farther into the room, a six-year-old with a long braid down her back walked up to Oliver with her hands on her hips. "Where have you been?"

"Hello to you, too, Susan."

"Why do you always call me Susan?"

"That's your name, isn't it?"

"You should call me Suzie."

"My apologies, but you are looking so grown up these days I can't help but call you by your full proper name."

She put a hand up to her mouth and snickered, then

got serious again. "Who's that?" she asked, looking suspiciously at Peter.

"That's Peter."

"Is he nice?"

"He's very nice."

"Hi, Peter."

"Hi, Suzie." Peter leaned down and shook her hand.

"I'm glad you're here, Oli. We brought chocolate chip cookies."

"Ooh, they're my favorite," Peter said.

Suzie grinned, swinging her arms at her side. "You want me to get you one?"

"I'd love one."

The girl dashed off toward the food table.

"Cute kid," Peter said.

"She is. She always takes time to talk to me every time I'm here."

Suzie skidded to a halt in front of Peter. "There you go." Then she took a big side step so she was in front of Oliver. "Here's yours."

"Thank you very much," he said, then took a bite. "These are good."

"I helped make them," Suzie said. "Oli, are you coming to church the Sunday before Christmas?"

Oliver pressed a finger on his chin in reflection. "*The Sunday before Christmas.* Uh, I'm not sure. That's several months from now. I might be working."

"On Sunday? You should rest on Sunday. It says so in the Bible."

"Do you always rest on a Sunday?"

Suzie squished her mouth to the side in thought.

"One time my mom and dad made me clean my room, and sometimes I have to play with my baby brother." She scrunched up her face. "That kinda feels like work."

"Well, I sure hope you don't quote scripture at your mom and dad when that happens."

Her eyes widened dramatically. "No way. I'd get in trouble."

"Get in trouble for what?" asked a tall, lean man who walked up behind Suzie. "She's not giving you grief, is she?"

"She always gives me grief. I think she makes it her mission to keep me in line. How have you been, Steve? How's business?"

"Busy, but good. It's good to see you."

"It's good to be here."

She tugged on her dad's elbow. "He has to come on the Sunday before Christmas, though," Suzie pushed.

"That's very specific. What's happening?" Steve asked, ruffling her hair.

She growled and madly flattened her hands on the top of her head. "'Cuz the kids' church is singing a song. We've already started practicing."

"Oh my. That does make it an extra-special day," Oliver said. "I can't make any promises, but I will certainly try my best. I would hate to miss that."

An older lady with short, white curly hair pressed herself into the conversation, patting Oliver on the cheek. "Oliver, so good to see you. You still our most eligible bachelor?"

"No, Mrs. Henry. Never have been."

She laughed. "You're such a tease. And who's your friend?"

"This is Peter. He's visiting."

"Peter, how nice to meet you. Are you single?"

"Nope." He held up his ring finger. "Twenty-five years this year."

"Congratulations. Lucky lady."

"I tell her that all the time, I don't think she's convinced."

"I can see you and Oliver are both teases. Well, you two make sure you stay for a cup of tea and a cookie after the service." She squeezed her shoulders up to her ears with a dimpled grin, then moved off.

Suzie spotted a friend and ran off to play, and Steve moved in closer to Oliver and Peter. "Oli, I was praying for you the other night. Woke up in the middle of the night and couldn't get back to sleep until I did."

"Really? That's interesting to know."

"So there *is* something." Steve nodded. "You don't have to give me any details, but I just wanted you to know that God is not silent. I kept thinking about Job when everything went wrong and it seemed like God had turned his back on him. You need to remember that things are not always what they seem."

"Thank you. I knew I came here for a reason this morning."

As church started, Steve gave Oliver a pat on the arm and nodded to Peter before he went to join his family.

"There you go," Peter said as they took a seat

toward the back where they could monitor the room. "Don't get distracted by the circumstances."

Peter remained standing as the music started, but Oliver sat, leaning his elbows on his knees with his eyes closed.

The acoustics in the church were far from performance appropriate, but to Oliver, they were perfect. He loved the echoey walls that multiplied the voices until they filled the entire room to overflowing. He didn't care what songs they sang, or who sang off-key. It was the spirit that was always in the place. It was one of the reasons he needed to be there that morning. When that little church sang to God, they meant it. The genuine worship always eased the burdens that he struggled to let go of. And that morning was no different.

Chapter 13

OLIVER HAD SAID goodbye to Peter, who had business to take care of in the city, and he leaned his head back against the elevator wall, letting out a slow, relaxed breath as it ascended. It was the first time he felt like he could see a positive end to everything.

He whistled a random tune as he entered his apartment and dropped his jacket over a chair, then went to check on Morgan's progress, knocking lightly on her door with a knuckle. When she didn't respond, he knocked harder, but still there was nothing, so he tried the knob and found it unlocked.

He knocked again as he pushed open the door. "Morgan?"

He poked his head in and saw her on her feet in front of the computer, dancing.

She had chunky headphones on and first hummed, then sang a couple of lyrics, then hummed again. Her vocals had a lilting quality that gave them an eerie beauty.

He bit his lip to restrain his smile and took a few steps into the room, ignoring the voice in his head that said it was probably more appropriate to back out. Catching her like this was so unexpected, he found it impossible to look away. It was the first time he'd seen her carefree. Previously, their interactions had carried an intensity most likely caused by the circumstances, but their own baggage would have added its own weight. It was nice to know the day had brought them both a break from the worries of the world.

He walked slowly toward her, expecting her to turn around at any moment. It wasn't long before she did.

Jumping backward, she fell against the table. If it hadn't been up against the wall, the monitors would have been knocked to the floor.

She ripped the headphones off. "What are you doing in here?"

"I just got home and wanted to see how things were coming along." He struggled to hold back his laugh.

"You could have knocked."

"I did. Several times. I wasn't trying to sneak up on you. It just … You were … " He gestured toward her with his hand. " … It was … " He wasn't usually lost for words. "It was nice to see you enjoying yourself," he finally managed to get out.

"Well … Thanks, but now I'm just mortifyingly embarrassed."

"You shouldn't be. You've got good moves."

She groaned. "Shut up. You're making it worse. I need to listen to music when I'm stuck on a job. It helps me to get unstuck."

"And the dancing?"

"Yes, the dancing too. And depending on how long you were there ... the singing as well."

"I enjoyed the singing."

She grabbed a wooden coaster off the table in front of her and threw it at him.

He batted it away, laughing. "So you're stuck then?"

She hid her own laugh behind a sigh. "Go away and come back in an hour and I'll know more. And don't be surprised if the door's locked."

He bowed his head and left, closing the door silently.

With the wall now between them, Oliver's smile dissolved. He had indulged in the moment, but it was a foolish thing to do, especially after such a good morning. All he had accomplished was to feed the attraction he felt for her and if he wasn't careful, he'd end up torturing himself over it. He knew he could never have her and would have to work harder on his self-control before someone got hurt.

<hr />

An hour later, Oliver knocked loudly on the door and waited. He didn't even check to see if it was locked. He wouldn't dare touch the door handle without her say-so. The thought brought a smile to his face that he quickly quashed.

"Come in," Morgan called out.

"You sure it's safe?" he yelled through the door, louder than necessary.

"Shut up," she growled. "Sorry, I didn't mean that,"

she added after he entered. "This system is impenetrable from the outside. They're good. And that's saying something."

"They should be," he said as he leaned over her shoulder to look at what she was doing. "They're experts at this stuff."

She turned to him, then quickly looked back at the screen and swallowed. He smelled really good, and she was finding it hard to breathe.

She scooted sideways to give him more room. "I understand they're good, but so am I." She could still smell him. "You want a drink?" she asked, escaping into the kitchen.

"I feel like a guest in my own home," he said, sitting on the couch.

"Good, maybe you won't walk in uninvited anymore."

"Touché. I am actually really sorry about that."

"It's fine. I'll survive. Drink?"

"No thanks."

"By the way," she said, filling a glass with water, "I forgot to ask how church was this morning."

"It was fantastic. I forget how much I miss it while I'm away." He leaned back on the arm of the couch and put a foot up on the cushion.

"The foster parents I lived with for a little while when I was a girl, Gramma and Grampa Mac, they brought me a few times."

"Gramma and Grampa Mac?"

"Yeah. They were an older couple and their last name was Macrae."

"Never went back?"

Morgan shrugged. "No one else I stayed with went. And by the time I was old enough to go on my own, it wasn't something I was interested in." She sat on the other end of the couch. "I remember going to kids' church in the basement of this old building that smelled like mildew. It was always cold and had a threadbare carpet. I would challenge myself every week to discover what color it was, but I could never decide if it was green or gray or brown."

"That's deep."

She gave him a look that included narrowing her eyes and then continued. "We would sit on that dingy carpet and this lady, Miss Richardson, would tell Bible stories using a felt board that she said was over fifty years old, which wasn't surprising since most of the bits were the same indistinguishable color as the carpet. But she was such a great storyteller, I didn't care. Then, at the end, before we finished, she'd ask the group if anyone wanted to ask Jesus into their heart. I'm pretty sure that was only for my benefit. I think the others had done it already. They were all regulars as far as I knew."

"And did you?"

"You know, it was strange. I wanted to, but I just couldn't understand how Jesus was supposed to fit into my heart and what it was he planned to do there besides change its color. So, no, I never did."

"Change its color?"

"Yeah. From red to white. I get it now, but back then I think I was a little worried he was going to remove all the blood or something."

"How long did you attend there?"

"Well … " she said, tucking her foot underneath her.

"Whoa, should I settle in? It looks like you're about to share an epic tale."

"Oh, yeah. It's fully epic."

"Please, continue."

"Okay, so there was a girl there about my age, Annie Greaves. Funny how you can remember names. I remember her name and the teacher's name, but I can't remember anyone else. Not even what they looked like. But I remember Annie and she always wore pink frilly dresses that made me so jealous."

"Terrible."

"I know, right? I would have given anything to have a pink frilly dress. Anyway, she didn't like me very much and used to tease me when the teacher wasn't looking. Then one morning, Miss Richardson was telling the story of Peter. Peter? The one who was killing all the Christians and then was blinded by a flash and fell off his horse?"

"Paul."

"Oh, okay, Paul. She was telling that story, and I remember thinking how crazy scary that would have been, and Annie started tugging at my braids.

"Now, you need to understand that Gramma Mac had to work hard to make those braids 'cause she had arthritis, and I was so proud of them because no one had ever braided my hair before. So Annie was tugging them and I really wanted to hear what happened to Paul, but she wouldn't stop. So I swung my arm around behind me to get her to stop, but I didn't realize her face was so close."

Oliver's eyes widened. "You didn't."

"I did. Popped her right in the nose. That pink dress was covered in bright-red blood before I even turned around. And I kid you not, my first thought was that she had red blood and not white, so she must not really be a Christian."

Oliver covered his laugh so she could continue.

"I can't say I felt bad. At least not until I found out they'd asked Gramma and Grampa Mac not to bring me to kid's church anymore.

"They kept me in the main service the next Sunday, but I wasn't happy, and I became a tad disruptive. From then on, because the church had two services, one of them would go, while the other stayed home with me. I never did find out what happened to Paul."

"You never thought to look it up?"

"Are you kidding? Have you seen the Bible? There are a lot of words in there. I'd have no idea where to start."

"True. Would you like to know?"

Morgan was unprepared for the leap in her stomach and the tears that tightened her throat. She shrugged it off. "I always thought maybe the Christians found him blind and beat him up. Gave him a taste of his own medicine."

"Judging by some of the Christians I know, there were probably a few who might have, but no. Paul became a Christian himself and joined the rest of them."

"No way. But he was so against them."

"Yeah, but when Jesus pays you a visit — and blinds you — you pay attention. Paul just wanted to serve God, so when he discovered Jesus was God, he had a turnaround."

"Huh. So how'd the other Christians take it? They must have been pretty freaked out."

"They were terrified, but they worked it out. You can read for yourself if you want. I've got a Bible on the bookshelf. I can open it to the right spot, or you could just Google it."

"Maybe some other time."

Oliver didn't push it. "It sounds like those foster parents were pretty special."

"They were, yeah. But it was only a couple months later that Gramma Mac had a stroke and Grampa Mac couldn't look after me himself, so they moved me on." She twisted the heart ring on her index finger. "He gave me this," she said, indicating the ring. "Gramma Mac wore it on a necklace because it wouldn't fit over her arthritic fingers. It was a ring he had given her when they were dating. Like a promise ring or something."

"What a beautiful memento. But that must have been such a hard time for you."

"They were the only truly good people I ever stayed with."

"You know, there's a little girl at my church, probably about the same age you were. Maybe a bit younger. She's what you might call precocious, but she's got a mom and dad who are raising her well and love her and she's in a secure environment. I can't imagine what it would have been like for you."

"I learned from a very young age that if you want anything in life, you have to work really hard and get it yourself. What I didn't know yet was that then, someone can frame you for a crime you didn't commit, and all your hard work dissolves into dust."

"I'm sorry."

"Doesn't matter." She slapped her hands on her lap. "What *does* matter is we need to figure out how to get into the system at Potters."

"I thought you said you can't."

"I can't get in from the outside, no. But there are other ways. It just depends on how much leeway your conscience gives you."

"No, it depends on how much leeway I believe Raquel has given me."

"That's a handy way around."

"I'm not trying to get around anything. I can honestly say that I think if there were any way to get in there, she would want you to give it a go. They'll have a record of it they can use to improve their security."

"Well, I can write a program that I can then upload onto their system that will open a door for me from here. All I need is a terminal connected to that network. But if your friend wants to know how genuine the possibility of a security breach is, then we can't ask for her assistance."

There was a sparkle in her eye that made Oliver want to give her the world. "I might have an idea of how to get you inside," he said.

Chapter 14

MORGAN RAN her hands down the sides of the purple dress as she stood on the pedestal. The skirt, made up of layers of tulle, was shorter in the front than the back, while pearl beading and stone embellishments covered the strapless bodice. This was the first dress she'd tried on that gave her the full range of motion, which was one reason it was now at the top of her list.

She tipped her head from one side to the other. The color looked amazing with her red hair, or so she thought. But she was no expert.

After hopping off the platform, she grabbed her phone, then jumped back up and sent a picture to Camilla.

She got a response almost immediately that had a variety of emojis and finished with a line of exclamation points. This was followed by:

> R you playing dress-up without me?????
> Who are you and what have you done
> with my Morgan!!!

> It's amazing what I'll put up with to stay
> alive. I need your advice. Does this color
> work?

> Honey, your life is in danger (skull emoji)
> and he's taking you on a hot date? Marry
> this guy at once (three heart emojis) ...
> also the color is perfect

> It's for work. I'll explain later

> Enjoy!!!!!!!!!

Morgan tossed the phone on her pile of clothes and twisted in front of the mirror again, rustling the fabric. She was finding the process of preparing for the approaching evening more stressful than the thought of breaking into an office at a party to infiltrate a business.

After Oliver had shared his plan about attending Raquel's function, he'd immediately organized to get her ready by booking her into the boutique a friend of his had suggested. He'd insisted she avoid looking at the price tag, but she couldn't resist. It made her stomach turn, and she had to remind herself that he made a lot more money than she did.

She ran her hand down the dress again, wondering if it could be returned.

"You okay in there?" Peter said from the other side of the heavy velvet curtain.

"Uh, yeah." The spell was broken, and she stepped down to the floor. "Did you want to see?"

"If I'm allowed, yeah."

Morgan pushed through to the waiting area and twirled.

"Wow."

"You like it?"

"Yeah, you look" — he threw his arms up — "great. I mean. I wish I could wax more eloquently. If Jemi were here, she'd have a lot to say, I'm sure."

"Jemi?"

"My wife. Are you happy with it?"

"Yeah, I just — I don't know if I'm comfortable having Oliver pay for it."

"Can you afford to buy a dress like that?"

"No, but — "

Peter put a hand up. "Hey, it's a business gig. And I can tell you right now that even if you *could* buy it, Oliver would never let you, because this is his thing, not yours."

"It's just so extravagant."

"The price tag or the dress?"

"Both."

"I'm going to hazard a guess that you've never attended one of these shindigs before?"

Morgan huffed. "I didn't even attend my prom."

"Then believe me when I tell you that your dress needs to be stunning. You might feel self-conscious now, but I promise you that if you go in anything less than that" — he punched his finger toward her — "you will stand out like a sore thumb."

"Okay, then I guess I'll take it."

"Great. That didn't take long at all. Where to next?"

Morgan closed her eyes and threw her head back in indignation. "I guess if a fancy dress is required, then I can't avoid the hair and makeup?"

"Not possible, no. And I have a feeling this next part will take longer than picking out the dress."

"I was afraid you'd say that. Sorry to drag you through all of this." Morgan scrunched her nose.

"Don't worry about me. One thing I've learned from my line of work is that I need to enjoy the downtime as much as the exhilaration of the action."

Morgan checked the time. "It's not for another hour and a half. You want to get something to eat? All this dressing up has made me hungry."

"Girl after my own heart."

"Can we go to the park? It's a beautiful day."

"I'd love to, but security is tricky. There is a nice place nearby though. A little hole-in-the-wall burger place Oliver took me to once. I think you'll like it."

Oliver glanced sideways at his new security detail as he was driven into the parking garage at his office. He couldn't tell whether Liam was taking this job very seriously, or if he was always this uncomfortably intense. Peter hadn't given him any details besides the fact that he chose Liam specifically to get a read on Oliver's employees.

"So, Liam. How long have you worked for Peter?"

Liam's eyes shifted briefly to Oliver before replying. "I don't work for him anymore. This is a favor he called in."

"Right. That makes sense."

"What does?"

"The way you're acting. You don't want to be here. Am I'm interrupting something?"

"Sir?"

"You just seem wound up, that's all."

"I'm concentrating. Would you rather I didn't?"

"Is it business or personal?"

"Sir?"

"The thing that I interrupted. Was it another job? Or was it something personal?"

Liam parked the car and shifted his body around to turn his attention to Oliver. "I don't believe that has any relevance to this operation."

"You're right. I'm sorry. I just find it strange that Peter would request that you leave something you'd already committed to."

Liam's lips puckered. "Peter has a way of believing he knows what's best."

Oliver nodded. "He does. But then, I've found that he's usually right."

Liam put a hand up. "Listen, I'm here to do a job, not make friends. No offense."

"No, of course."

When the two men reached Oliver's office, Oliver asked Liam to wait outside while he made a private phone call. By the look on Liam's face, the call was no surprise.

Oliver dialed Peter's number. "Hey, Peter. You guys getting on okay?"

"Have you ever been in one of those fancy dress places?"

Oliver stretched his free arm across his chest and looked out the window. "Can't say that I have."

"It smells weird."

Oliver laughed. "So everything's going as planned, then?"

"We're on target. Dress has been chosen, and we're headed for a bite to eat before we enter enemy territory, aka the salon."

"Roger that. Hey, this Liam guy you've stuck me with — "

"Is he giving you a hard time?"

"He's fine, just a little moody."

"I was afraid of that. I took the risk because he's the right man for the job, and I needed to change his environment."

"Yeah, he doesn't seem real keen to be here."

Peter sighed. "No, he's not. I should have warned you."

"He said he owed you a favor."

"I had to use my trump card, which I only use in emergencies."

"So he's in trouble?"

"Something like that. His dad just passed away about a month ago, and it sent him into a spiral. He got in touch last week after I hadn't heard from him in over a year. He was in trouble and needed me to bail him out, which I can assure you is very unlike him. He's not a man who asks for help."

"But I take it he was one of your guys at one point?"

"Yeah, I got my hands on him when he was twenty. He was a rough diamond — a very rough diamond. But he had a way of reading the room or a situation. He always saw stuff I didn't and could tell when a fight was coming. It's something of an art form for him."

"Was he with you long?"

"Long enough to feel like family. I remember the first time he learned I was a Christian. He was so mad at me." Peter laughed. "It messed him up big-time."

"Why?"

"'Cause he could read something on me that he couldn't understand. He was drawn to it, so when he found out what *it* was, I think he was mortified. His background is not aboveboard and the guilt started getting to him when he was around me.

"But after he got used to the idea of my faith, he became very receptive to the gospel. He especially liked the stories of when the Pharisees tried to trap Jesus with their questions."

"But something happened?"

There were layers of disappointment in Peter's sigh. "Something always happens. He went on a mission with another guy. It was supposed to be surveillance, but his partner saw an opportunity to take out the enemy, so he set a bomb. He told Liam to give him a signal for when to blow it, but Liam refused because it wasn't what they were there for. The guy set off the bomb anyway and ended up killing two kids. Liam was furious with him."

"No kidding. Did he feel responsible?"

"That wasn't the problem. I mean, he did feel partly responsible, but that wasn't what chased him off.

"When something like that happens, when a mission goes wrong, we always fully investigate it. We talk to those involved, separately, and get both sides of the story. Liam, as I said, took responsibility for his part. But his partner wasn't cut from the same cloth, and he laid all the blame squarely on Liam's shoulder. I wasn't there when it went down, and Liam ended up being severely reprimanded. By the time I was informed about the situation, it was too late. He took off before I had the chance to sort it all out, and I didn't hear much from him for several years after that."

"Until he got into trouble."

"Right. I won't get into the specifics on his father except to say that I'm trying to protect him from making bad choices while he's grieving the loss of someone who's mistreated him."

"Thanks for filling me in."

"He just needs to remember who he really is, and that he's better off being around people who value him."

"I'll see what I can do. Have fun at the salon." Oliver laughed.

"I think my current mission is more intimidating than that firefight you and I got caught in just outside of Benghazi."

"You'll be fine. Just make sure you don't shoot anything."

"Roger that."

Chapter 15

MORGAN BREATHED out a happy sigh when they entered the restaurant Peter had chosen. Eating a greasy burger would help her recalibrate after feeling like a fraud at the high-end fashion boutique.

"We'll have to make it quick 'cause we still have to get across town," Peter said.

After collecting their meals, Morgan put a hand on Peter's arm to stop him. "Wait, let me pick the table." She noted the exits and windows before focusing in on a table in the corner. She pointed. "That one."

"Hey, look at you. You'll be an expert in no time."

"I've been learning from the best." They both sat and dug into their meals.

"So, Jemi is an unusual name," Morgan said as she lifted her burger to her mouth. "Is that short for something?"

"Jemila."

"I've never heard that before. Is she American?"

"No, she's Middle Eastern."

"Really? Is there an interesting story there? Or did you two just meet at college or something?"

Peter laughed. "No, there is definitely an interesting story there. We met when I was on a mission during Desert Storm."

"You're kidding."

"Nope." Morgan nodded her head for him to go on as she took another bite causing sauce to drip down her hand. "Oh, you want to hear about it?"

"Mmm-hphm." She licked at the sauce.

"Well, I was young and stupid and thought I could save the world with my own two hands." Peter cracked his knuckles. "I was the only one on that mission without a sweetheart, and I thought that made me the luckiest guy in the world."

"Oh, I hear you on that one. That would be tough."

"Yeah. These guys had pictures of their wives or girlfriends, kids if they had them. I saw what it did to them. How hard it was for them every single day. I was so glad I didn't carry around that baggage, and I was convinced that there was no woman in the world that could tempt me to put that kind of pressure on myself. I was happy being carefree."

"And then Jemi turned up?"

"And then Jemi turned up."

"So was it love at first sight?"

Peter choked on his drink. "No. It's not that kind of love story."

"More of a *friends-to-lovers* kind?"

"More like *enemies* to lovers, I'd say."

Morgan leaned forward. "The best kind."

"Is it though?"

They both laughed. "Makes for a good story anyway. So spill. Was she a soldier or something?"

"Oh, no. She was as tough as one, though. But like I said, I was on a mission. We'd gotten intel about a base where we could gain access to a fiber optic cable that linked Scud missile launchers to Iraqi command and control. Our mission was to destroy that cable. What we didn't know was that they had taken a group of women hostage."

Morgan had her burger poised in front of her mouth but paused. "Don't tell me Jemi was one of these women."

"She certainly was."

"Were they hostages because they'd done something? Or just because they were women."

"They were hiding Bible verses in these little paper beads. They'd string a bunch on a necklace, and that was how they smuggled the Bible into places where it was illegal. Not only that, but Jemi had also begun gathering intel on the Iraqis and sending that to an American base."

"Using the beads?"

"That's right. The Iraqis found out, and that's why they took her and the other women. I didn't know that at the time, obviously."

"So you saved them."

"Oh boy, don't let Jemi hear you say that. She was so mad when we turned up."

"What?"

"Yeah, we messed up her escape plan. We turned up in

139

our gear. Top guys in our field. The experts. And we ran into this group of women, dirty and weak from being mistreated. Jemi was leading them in their escape. But me and my boys, we had a job to do, and even though we wanted to help, we were afraid they'd give up our position."

"And they were afraid you'd give up theirs?"

"Perceptive. But we were the ones with the guns and the training, so in my book, that meant we were in control."

"Jemi didn't agree."

He let out a burst of laughter. "She thought I was an arrogant fool who was going to get us all killed."

Morgan grinned. "Were you?"

Peter shrugged. "Depends on who you ask. But yes, she may have been right about the arrogant part. When I refused to tell her why we were there, she slapped me and we had the biggest, quietest argument I've ever had in my life. She was the most stubborn woman I'd ever met. Still is."

"I think I would like Jemi."

"Oh, you definitely would. She's quite a woman. In the end we were running out of time, so we had to work together, but neither one of us was happy about it."

"So after all of that, how'd you get Jemi to fall in love with you?"

Peter looked at his watch. "Oh, look at the time. We should get going."

"Are you kidding? You can't do that to me."

"I'll tell you one day, but right now, all I'll say is that there is a fine line between love and hate. Now, let's go."

Morgan had finished her lunch, but Peter had barely eaten any of his. He finished it in a few quick bites before he stood.

"Did you learn that skill in the army?" She laughed as she threw her garbage in the trash.

"That, my friend, has taken years of training to master. If you're lucky, I might teach you one day."

"No thanks, I like to taste my food."

"Good morning, everyone." Oliver addressed his team. "By now you've all had the chance to meet Liam who approached me recently about partnering with us here at Wright and Lavigne and asked for the opportunity to speak with a few of us separately to get a feel for how things work."

"That's highly unusual," said Carl.

Liam spoke up. "You expect me to trust my money to people I know nothing about?"

Liam's interaction with the group so far had been an equal measure of skepticism and haughtiness. Oliver was impressed at his ability to play the part of a sly businessman better than those in attendance. If his skill at reading a room was of the same caliber, Liam would be an excellent asset to have on his team.

"He won't keep you long, but I'd like us all to cooperate as I believe this could be a highly profitable partnership." That should quiet a few arguments. "Carl, you can be up first."

Arthur entered the room, rapping a knuckle on the door frame.

"Late as usual," Carl grumbled. "All right. Let's get this over with." He stood. "Are we staying in here?"

"No, I can meet each of you in your respective offices," Liam said, then turned his attention to Arthur, who had sidled up next to Oliver. The others got up from the table and left.

"What's this all about?" he asked after giving Liam a once-over.

"I was going to catch you before the meeting," Oliver said

"Yeah, sorry I was late. I had some important stuff to do."

"Liam's my security detail. He's trying to gather information to see what he can find out. Have you discovered anything?"

Arthur looked at Liam again. "I haven't had time. But this is a pretty tight ship. I think you may be looking in the wrong place."

"Well, Liam comes highly recommended. If there's anything to find, he'll find it."

Liam stood. "Arthur." He shook Arthur's hand while pinning him with his eyes. He gripped the other man's hand longer than necessary, then let go and turned to Oliver. "I'll see you later."

Arthur watched him go then let out a quiet chuckle. "Wow. He's full of himself."

"I don't care if he's full of himself. I just care if he's good at his job, which I'm assured he is."

"It's your life, Oli. Just make sure you know who you

can trust." Arthur slapped him on the back before leaving.

When he was left alone, Oliver pressed his hands onto the top of the table and hung his head. It was highly probable that at least one person from that meeting wanted him dead. He'd looked them all in the eye, but for each inclination that something was off, he had a reasonable excuse.

Even though his relationship with most of them wasn't great, the idea that one of them had made a plan to kill him was a bitter pill to swallow. Peter was right to bring Liam in. Oliver needed someone from the outside to come in and do the heavy lifting when it came to discerning what was going on. Oliver was too close, but he hoped that what Arthur said was right. If it turned out to be outside the office somehow, even with his life still in danger, it would be a weight off his mind.

If Morgan had the skill to hack into his business, then it was realistic to believe that someone else had as well. And if that was the case, they could have planted the emails to throw everyone off. But that scenario only brought up more questions.

God, you're the only one who knows what's really going on here. Whatever is hiding, bring it out of the shadows and into the light.

Morgan puffed up her cheeks and let out a slow, noisy breath. It was the second time in only a few weeks that she found herself in front of a large salon mirror. Her hair was styled in an elegant wave and now it was time for the makeup, but she was already worn out, with the evening still to come.

"Remember, natural," she said to the flawless woman who had pulled up a stool.

"Got it."

Morgan faced the mirror and watched cynically as the woman applied various levels of makeup, some of which had no obvious purpose that Morgan could discern. But if this was what it took to get the job done, then she'd endure.

It wasn't that makeup was new to her. She usually wore a small amount when she left the house, but she expected today's application to be thick and uncomfortable. A comparable experience to how she felt about the whole day.

The woman attempted to engage in conversation, but Morgan couldn't cooperate. Instead of focusing on the discomfort of her current experience, her mind wandered to the night ahead. She trusted Oliver but had no idea what to expect about the party, and tried to imagine what it would be like so she would be prepared.

The job itself was simple, but after spending the last three years in prison, a tremor kept randomly twitching through her body at the thought of going back there. She had been ready to hack into Potter's without their permission, but when it really came down to it, she was grateful that Oliver had taken precautions to make sure, if caught, she should be safe.

Should be.

Chapter 16

OLIVER WAS on a phone call when Liam knocked on his open door. Oliver waved him in and finished his call.

"Come in. You all finished?"

"You've got an interesting bunch there," Liam said, plopping down into a chair across the desk and running a hand through his hair. "Brian hates your guts."

"Yeah, I know. He was loyal to my father and feels it's his duty to make sure I don't mess up the company. Not sure if he'd kill me to do it, though."

"No. I didn't get that from him either. But I'm not here to make that kind of assessment directly, just to gather information along with a bit of intuition and report to Peter."

"Anything else stand out?"

"I could make the argument that everyone here is hiding something."

"That's because they probably all are. Everyone has an angle."

"And that's the tricky part, weeding out the important secrets from the trivial ones."

"I guess that's what you're here for."

"Yeah."

"Anyone actually on my side, you think?"

"I know I make it sound depressing, but there are a few, yes. They might not agree with all of your decisions, but I have crossed some off the list."

"So besides Brian, who else is suspicious?"

"Eve, for one."

"Really? I can't see her being involved."

"She's not the mastermind behind it if she's involved. But she basically refused to talk about you at all. Avoided mention of you like the plague. It could simply mean she has a crush on you, but it's definitely something."

"She's married."

"Yes, she said that. Several times, in fact. Like she was apologizing."

"And what does that mean?"

"Like I said, she could just have a crush. Or she's tried to kill you, and she doesn't want to give it away. But again, this is all conjecture at this point."

"Right. I'm not used to having enemies in my own territory. I mean dangerous ones. But I also wanted to ask you — Do you think it's possible that the threat is completely outside my company?"

"Sure, but honestly, I find it more likely that there is a connection within. That would be an awful lot of trouble to go through. There are easier ways. More often than not, there's a connection — Oh, by the way, I haven't met with Arthur yet."

"Don't worry about him. He's on our side."

"You do realize he's got narcissistic sociopathic tendencies?"

"Arthur? How do you figure that?"

"It's not all that uncommon in men with power, and it doesn't mean he's a killer. I just thought you should know."

"Arthur and I have been friends for a long time."

"Speak of the devil," Liam said with a smile when he caught sight of Arthur entering.

Arthur's eyebrows lifted. "I was just coming to see how everything went. I assume that's okay with you?"

"Yeah, sure, come on in." Liam waved him over. "I've been meaning to ask you, Arthur. You see your parents much?"

"That's an odd question. Have you discovered that we're looking for someone with a bad relationship with his parents or something?" Arthur quipped.

"No, nothing like that. It's more of a game."

"A game." He looked at Oliver, who shrugged. "Okay, well, I don't have a very intriguing answer to give you. I see them most years around Christmas because they live in Florida, and my job here is very demanding. I love my parents, but if I'm honest, I love this job more. I've committed to it and I wouldn't want to let Oliver down."

"Thanks."

"Did I win?"

"No. This is the type of game that I always win."

Arthur's jaw flexed, and he kept eye contact with Liam but spoke to Oliver. "You sure you want to get into bed with this guy?"

"Well," Liam said, looking at his watch. "I think we should head out, Oliver. You have that other engagement to get ready for."

"What other engagement?" Arthur asked.

"Sorry, that's confidential." Liam stood, and Arthur stepped up to him. "Is there something further I can help you with?" Liam's voice was casual, but his manner was not.

"No, but, Oliver, I think you can do better than this guy. I could probably do better than this guy."

"Step down, Arthur. This has been entertaining, to say the least, but I do have to get going. And I'm sure you have work to do."

"Suit yourself. You know where to find me if this guy screws you over."

"Thanks."

On the drive home, Oliver was fidgeting. Liam noticed, but waited for Oliver to speak first.

Finally, Oliver couldn't hold it back anymore. "I've never seen Arthur act that way before."

"That's because you've never seen him challenged."

"What was that question about his parents for?"

"Random question that served several purposes. The biggest of which was to tell him he lost, and I won. It was at that point that he lost his cool. When you lose your cool, your tongue often gets loose."

"What else did the question reveal?"

"That he obviously believes his position within the company is indispensable, that you can't do without him, and if he went away, then Wright and Lavigne would be sunk."

"You got all that from what he said?"

"No, not just that. My whole interaction with him. He didn't like me being there, but it goes further than that. I can't really explain it."

Oliver nodded. "Hey, thanks for all you did in there today. It was really important to me. I think your input is going to help. I'm glad Peter brought you in on this one."

Liam's hands tightened on the wheel. "We've had such a good day. Don't do this."

"Do what?"

"Peter asked you to give me support. But I don't need you to babysit me because I'm having a hard time. That's what Peter told you, right? Did he tell you my dad died, and I'm spiraling out of control?"

"Something like that."

"Listen, Oliver, I appreciate Peter's concern for me. He means a lot to me and that's the only reason I'm here, because I respect and trust him, but sometimes a man's gotta hurt and there's nothing you can do about it. It doesn't mean I'll do my job poorly, but it also doesn't mean I need fixing."

"Sorry, it's just that I know what it's like when a father you despise dies."

"I don't think you can compare your experience to mine."

Oliver pushed his tongue into his cheek. "Peter didn't give me the details of your relationship with your dad, but mine left me for dead."

Liam stopped the car at a red light and used the opportunity to focus on Oliver. "Your dad left you for dead?"

"Yeah."

"Are we talking figuratively?"

"Nope. When I was eleven. Nothing was ever the same after that."

Liam didn't speak again until they were moving. "My dad was a conman. He was good, too, and when he found out I had a bit of a knack, he started getting me involved."

"How old were you?"

Liam blew out a breath. "Not sure. Around ten, I guess."

"You enjoy it?"

"Oh, yeah, sure." Liam laughed. "That wasn't the problem. The problem was, my dad was so good at the con that he was able to load all the blame on me if we got caught. He said it was because I was a minor so I wouldn't get into as much trouble, and I guess he was right, but he got awfully good at the shocked face of a disappointed parent.

"Then when I got out of juvie, he would always berate me about what a bad kid I was. He loved making that scene. Said it was all for show, but I'm pretty sure he enjoyed doing it."

"Man, that's rough. It's funny how a man who's treated you that way can mess you up so much when he's no longer on the planet. When my dad died, I was wrecked for a while, so I know what you mean about needing to hurt. And I know you're not thrilled to be here, but I appreciate it. Not in a fixing-you kind of way, but genuinely. Peter knows how to pick the best. If he trusts you, so do I."

Liam nodded. "Good, then trust me when I say to watch out for Arthur. I'm not saying he's the man we're looking for, but I wouldn't put it past him to stab you in the back if he got a better offer."

Oliver shook his head. "I'll watch my back, but I really hope you're wrong about him. I've trusted Arthur with a lot of my business, and he's always been great at his job and a good friend."

"A good friend, huh? Well, that doesn't usually come with the narcissistic personality type. I hope for your sake I'm off base, but I'm not usually." He pulled into the parking space underground. "You've got Peter bringing you in tonight?"

"Yeah."

"Then I'll leave you here and start getting that report ready for him." Oliver opened the door but Liam stopped him. "Hey, just let Peter know I'll be okay. He won't believe it coming from me."

"*Will* you be okay?"

"I've made it this far, haven't I?"

Chapter 17

OLIVER CLEARED his throat as he tugged on the sleeves of his suit jacket, then held his breath, counting off until he needed to take a breath again. He'd been to plenty of these events, but never with a date, and as much as he told himself this wasn't a date, he was having trouble shaking the feeling.

His phone chirped to life, and he checked the message. It was from Morgan saying she was ready whenever he was.

He held his breath one more time, then went into the hall to knock on her door. She called for him to come in, but when he entered, she was nowhere to be found, so he closed the door and headed for the bookshelf to busy himself, not wanting to intrude on whatever last-minute thing she was doing.

He was scanning a shelf when he heard her heels on the bathroom tiles and he turned in time to see her enter the living room.

She stood just outside the hall and twisted slowly,

pulling at the sides of the skirt to exaggerate the motion. "What do you think?"

He allowed himself the opportunity to stare for only a couple of seconds. "Wow." He was surprised the word came out unhindered by the tightness in his throat.

"That's what Peter said." She smiled. "You look nice, too."

"But not 'wow'?" he questioned with a lifted eyebrow.

She felt a flush color her cheeks and hoped the makeup hid it. He did look great, but she wouldn't admit that to herself. "Meh," she said. "There's only so much you can do with a tux."

"True. You know, with so many options for dresses, I'm surprised to see you didn't choose pink."

"Purple is close enough. And it's frilly, so it still counts."

"Annie Greaves, eat your heart out."

She laughed, a deep sound that made him want to laugh too. But instead, he pulled his gaze away from her and focused on the window, walking over to it.

He watched her reflection walk up behind to join him.

"While we were out today, Peter told me the story about how he met his wife. Some of it anyway."

"It's a fascinating story. And Jemi is perfect for him. Keeps him in line. Just what he needs. Or needed. I think he's softened."

"That's the impression I got." Morgan sighed, a soft mewling sound. "So when do we leave?"

Oliver checked his watch. "Fifteen minutes. So, I

guess we should get down to business. I take it you have what you need to upload of the virus, or whatever it is that you made?"

She held up a small clutch. "Ready and waiting."

"Okay, good. Take a seat." He moved to sit on the edge of the chair with his elbows leaning on his knees. She walked carefully over to the couch, not confident in heels, and sat with her ankles crossed, surprised at how easily it came to her.

"Raquel likes to host these parties pretty often, so I've been to a few, and I know Potters' offices from visiting for work. They always host their events in a large open area past reception.

"When we enter the party, you'll see there is a hall to the right that will be out of view of everyone at the party. Once you head down that hall, the second office on the left belongs to a guy named John Silverman. He's good at his job, but he's also one of the sleaziest people I know, which will come in handy for us tonight as he always leaves his office unlocked at these parties."

"Why?"

"Because at some point or other he finds a woman to take in there."

"Oh. Gross."

"Tonight, it will be the only computer we can get access to. Now, how long do you expect it to take you?"

"My best estimate is five to ten minutes, assuming everything goes to plan."

"Great, that should be easy, then. I can keep an eye on him while you get in there and do what you need to do."

"Sounds easy enough."

Oliver caught a slight tremble in her voice. "You okay with all of this?"

She straightened her back and took a deep breath, pushing it out between her lips while running her hands along her skirt. "Mostly. I guess I'd just like to be aware of the consequences if I get caught."

"You have nothing to worry about. I'll tell Raquel everything. I can promise you she'll be on our side."

"I guess that's everything settled."

"Great. Shall we go?"

They both stood and moved for the door. Without thinking, Morgan slipped her arm through his and smiled up at him. Time froze for the briefest moment, but then, as if by silent agreement, they both turned and continued forward.

She kept her arm in his until they reached the elevator, only because if she removed it, it would have been obvious and awkward, but her stomach felt like it was on fire.

Peter noticed something was off when they got in the car but wasn't about to say anything.

"What's that stupid grin about?" Oliver asked as he buckled his seatbelt.

"Oh, that's nothing."

"Mm-hmm." Oliver decided he didn't want to know.

When they arrived at Potters, Oliver exited the car first, then opened the door for Morgan. "Thanks for the lift," he said to Peter.

"I've already debriefed their security, so if you have any problems, they'll be ready.

Morgan had been impressed by the foyer at the entrance to Potters building, but when Morgan and Oliver walked through the glass doors to the side of the reception area where the function was taking place, her chest tightened. Peter had been right about her attire, and she was glad she had access to his wisdom while shopping. Otherwise she would have bought something less suitable and would have turned around immediately and walked out.

The crowd was intimidating and gave her an excuse to push close to Oliver. It was the only place she felt safe at the moment. Her fear of any kind of intimacy with him was long gone.

"You okay?" he asked, taking her hand to give it a squeeze before letting go.

"Do I not look okay?" she asked with a touch of horror.

He grabbed her hand again and pulled her to the side. "Hey, you look beautiful. Just breathe. Once you've been here for a few minutes, you'll settle. I promise."

"Okay, yeah. I've just never been to anything like this before."

"You sure it's not nerves about your mission?"

"No way. I'm more at home in front of a computer. That will be the highlight of my night."

"You'll get your chance soon enough. But I need to find John first."

They remained on the edge of the multitude while Oliver took stock of the room. Then the crowd parted, and a woman who looked like she had been dipped in liquid gold approached, making sure her cleavage was to its best advantage. She stretched out her arms toward Oliver.

"Oli," she said, closing in on him and kissing his cheek. "It's so good to see you. I didn't realize you were bringing a date."

"No. I don't usually inform you of my plans."

She laughed demurely. "Maybe not, but perhaps I know you better than you think I do."

Oliver put a hand on Morgan's back. "Gillian, this is Morgan. She works with me."

"Ah, an employee. I always knew you were a generous guy. Morgan, what a special treat this must be for you. Getting to see how the other side lives. It's lovely to meet you."

"Yes, this is quite the party. You rich guys sure know how to put on a show."

Gillian smiled so her nose crinkled, and she slipped past Oliver, running a finger across his chest. "I'll find you later." Then she moved on to work the room.

Oliver shook his head. "She tries to get me to go home with her at every one of these things."

"So she's like the female version of John Silverman?"

"Something like that."

"Ever been tempted?"

"Maybe in my younger years, but not these days."

He shook his head. "I feel bad for her if I'm honest, the lengths she goes to get attention."

"A woman like that? I wouldn't imagine it would be hard for her to get what she wants."

"I think the problem is that she goes headlong after the things she can't have. I was at a Christmas party once where she jumped out of a cake."

"You're kidding. Was that for you?"

"No, there was a prince from some European country attending."

"Well, she might be desperate, but she's very beautiful. You sure you're not tempted?"

"Not my type. Can I get you something to drink?"

"I'll have whatever you have." Morgan watched him zigzag through the crowd and wondered if Oliver had a type. He'd made it quite clear when she got into his car after she'd saved his life that she wasn't it, but she had to admit, she was relieved to hear Gillian wasn't either.

She backed up closer to the wall while scanning the room and accidentally made eye contact with someone through the crowd. He immediately headed her way.

He was good-looking in a generic sort of way. It was obvious he looked after himself, but Morgan didn't like the way his eyes devoured her.

"Good evening, miss. Looks like you're playing the part of the wallflower tonight." He held out his hand to shake hers, but when she gave it to him, he lifted it to his lips. "My name's John."

"Morgan," she said, pulling her hand back when he didn't let go.

"I don't believe I've ever seen you at one of these

things before, which I forgive you for as you have made this party something extra special."

"She's with me," Oliver said, handing her a drink as he maneuvered between them.

John took a step back, obviously intimidated, even though there wasn't much of a size difference. "Oliver, how good to see you. She was standing here on her own. I didn't want her to feel ignored."

"Mm-hmm. How are you doing, John?" Oliver asked, taking a step closer to him so he had to move back farther.

"Wonderful as ever. You know how much I love these things. So many beautiful women." John winked at Morgan, but no one spoke, leaving an awkward silence that John felt compelled to fill. "Well, it was lovely to meet you, Morgan. Oliver." He nodded and went to find easier prey.

"Is that all anyone does at these parties? Try to pick people up?" Morgan said as she watched John until he disappeared.

"Isn't that what happens at most parties?"

"Good point. So I take it that was Mr. Silverman?"

"In the flesh."

Morgan took a sip of her drink, then lifted the glass to get a better look at it. "Do you always drink mineral water?"

"Not always. Sometimes I splash out and get a ginger ale."

"Is that because of God?"

He laughed. "Straight to the point, hey? But no, not

exactly. It's more to do with what alcohol did to my life several years ago."

"You had a thing for it then?"

"Not just a *thing*. I was in love with it."

"What was your poison of choice?"

"Anything expensive."

"Interesting. One of my foster moms was an alcoholic. Expensive definitely wasn't her thing."

Raquel was doing the rounds and hurried over to Oliver when she spotted him. "You made it."

"I did." Oliver leaned forward and kissed her cheek. "And I'd like you to meet Morgan. Morgan, this is Raquel."

"Oh, wonderful. Morgan, it is an absolute pleasure to meet you. I had a look at the report on your progress, although it doesn't look like you made much. I won't say I'm disappointed, but I was impressed with your method. Unfortunately for you, our system is unbreachable."

"Yes, well, it is a very good system, but all systems have their weaknesses." Morgan's gaze floated from Oliver to the hall and back to Raquel, who stood up a little straighter.

"I think you might be surprised to find that ours does not."

"We'll see."

"Oh? So, you haven't given up then?"

"I don't give up that easily, no."

Raquel's red lips twisted up into a wicked grin. "I like her, Oli. And I look forward to reading further reports. But for now, I'll leave you two. I've yet to get around to everyone."

Oliver ducked his head and laughed when Raquel twisted off to enter another conversation.

"What's so funny?" Morgan asked, elbowing him.

"You. Just like when you saved my life at the restaurant, you would never win a game of poker. If Raquel wasn't so certain of victory, you would have given our plan away."

"I guess I'm not as good a liar as you are," she said, mildly offended.

"She brought out your competitive streak, though, didn't she? I'm more confident than ever that we've got this."

"Oh, I've definitely got this. Let me know when you're ready so I can get some actual work done."

"Finish your drink, then I'll monitor John."

Oliver was right. After Raquel's comments, Morgan was fired up and ready to show Raquel that they weren't impervious to hackers.

She swigged down her drink, her eyes watering as the bubbles burned her throat. Then she placed her glass on a passing tray. "Let's go then."

"You're keen."

"Of course I am. It's not just Raquel. I want this whole thing over and done with. I'm not into this whole — " She flitted her hand around but couldn't come up with a suitable word. "Party thing."

"Party thing," Oliver said. "Okay then, let's get started."

Morgan circled around toward the hall, keeping an eye on Oliver until he got into position and gave her a nod.

Chapter 18

ONCE MORGAN MOVED out of sight, Oliver squeezed through the crowd, chatting with different people but always keeping an eye on John.

Simon, a Potters employee whom Oliver had met a few times, caught his eye and lifted a finger in greeting. "Hey, Oliver. I hear things are coming along with this project you've brought us."

"Yeah, it's, uh." Oliver grabbed an hors d'oeuvre from a passing tray, glancing again at his mark, who was currently surrounded by a crowd of people who were laughing at a joke he must have told. "Yeah, it's good."

"Good? Do I detect a little deviation from that original passion you had? Last time I spoke to you about it, you were gushing."

"Well, I can only do so much gushing."

"Yeah, I guess that's how these things go. Everyone is excited at the start but then it turns into just another job."

"No, don't get me wrong. I'm still excited about it. It

looks like we'll be able to help a lot of people." He turned and caught the back of John as he made his way to the bar.

Oliver looked at Simon. "Will you excuse me? I've just seen someone I need to speak to."

Simon gave him an odd look but nodded and turned to join another conversation.

Having lost sight of John, Oliver wound through the crowd but stopped abruptly when his jacket caught on something. He twisted to unhook it from whatever it was snagged on, but discovered Gillian's hand had found its way into his pocket.

"Oli, I was hoping I'd find you on your own. Did your date have to leave?"

"No, she's, uh, in the bathroom. Listen, Gillian, I —"

"I'm worried about you, Oli." She pouted. "Don't tell me you're breaking all the rules and having an office romance. You do know how dangerous those things are, don't you? One wrong move and you'll be slapped with a sexual harassment suit. Not smart. Besides, wouldn't you rather be with someone more … experienced? I mean, she's pretty in a girlish sort of way, but —"

"I happen to think she's very beautiful. But we aren't involved." He felt compelled to make that clear, not for Gillian's sake, but for his own.

"Oh?"

Oliver twisted around but couldn't see John. "If you'll excuse me."

She grabbed hold of his arm. "Oh, Oli. I'm feeling a bit dizzy all of the sudden. I'm sorry I —"

Oliver took her weight as she fell into him, then lowered her to the ground. She groaned and reached for him, holding on with surprising strength. "Oli, stay with me."

The crowd formed a circle and several phones were perched high above them for the best view.

Raquel kneeled down beside him. "Is she okay? What happened?"

"She said she was dizzy and fainted. Maybe you should call an ambulance. I don't know how serious it is." He knew it was an act and needed to bring a resolution quickly because right now he was more concerned with finding John than with making sure Gillian understood he couldn't be manipulated.

Gillian blinked her eyes up at him. "Oli, is that you? I'm frightened."

He tried to extract her hands from him, but all he did was make her grip tighter.

"Gillian, you need to let go. Just lie back and rest."

"You won't go?"

"I'll call the ambulance."

"No. I don't think I need an ambulance. I'm feeling better." She used Oliver to claw her way into a sitting position, then put a hand on his face. "Could you help me to a chair?"

He lifted her easily and half carried her to a couch against the wall.

"I'll get you some water," he said, pulling her arms off his neck.

"Hurry back."

He pulled Raquel aside. "She'll be fine. Just let her sit there and recover." He didn't have time to explain.

"Don't tell me this is another cake incident."

"I thought you were overseas for that party?"

"I was, but that kind of news travels. Where's Morgan wandered off to?"

He scanned the room. "Oh, she's probably getting chatted up somewhere around here. I better go see if I can find her. She might need saving."

"Good thinking."

Oliver hurried to get another view of the room. He scrutinized every corner, but he couldn't find John.

Morgan cast her eyes around the office to get her bearings.

Signed sports paraphernalia filled a shelf on one wall and a large abstract painting hung on another. She studied it for a second, trying to work out what the shapes were creating, then she tipped her head sideways and squinted. After a moment, the picture came together and her cheeks reddened. She jerked her head away, abandoning her inspection to focus on the computer.

While it was booting, she inserted the USB. She'd included a program to help override the password protection. Most security hinged on not letting people in from the *outside*. Hacking into a computer at the terminal offered less resistance.

Her fingers scrambled across the keys. "Come on,"

she mumbled, then bit her lip. "Come on — Yes." She pumped a fist in triumph. "Raquel is going to be so mad."

She logged into the back end of the system. The intensity of concentration was momentarily replaced by a smile. It was the first time that day that she felt like she was in her own skin.

After beginning the upload, she kept her hand on the USB, not wanting to waste another second more than was necessary. It was one thing to get caught in an unattended office, but it was another to be found tampering.

Her eyes bandied between the door and the upload progress. With only a minute or two left, the seconds dragged and her heart raced.

When the transfer was finally complete, she shut down the computer and skirted around the desk, letting out a laughing breath that caught in her throat when the door opened.

There was a split second when she thought Oliver had come to retrieve her, but instead, John stepped through the door and closed it behind him.

His hand pressed on the handle, a gesture to prove it was fully closed.

"Morgan. When I saw you step away from the party, I had my hopes. But I'd be lying if I didn't say I'm surprised to see you here. My reputation obviously precedes me."

Morgan swallowed. "No, I'm sorry. It's not what you think. I was looking for the bathroom."

"Oh, you want to do a little role-play?" He put his

bottom lip between his teeth and nodded. "I'm up for that." He slunk toward her. "I'm sorry, miss. Maybe I can help you."

Morgan moved behind a set of chairs, keeping them as a barrier. "No, I'm serious. I got lost. I'm sorry for intruding in your personal space. I'll get out of your way."

He faked a move one way and then went the other. She made a break for the door and he grabbed her arm. She wrenched away, but it forced her off balance, and she tripped, twisting her ankle before pitching to the ground.

He slid down on top of her. "Don't worry, I'll be gentle."

The door opened, and Oliver's frame filled the space. In one swift motion, he grabbed John by the collar and flipped him off Morgan.

John scrambled to stand. "Oliver, hey. I found her in here. I had nothing to do with it. When I came in, she was already here."

Oliver stepped across the space and punched John in the face, then turned his attention back to Morgan. She was attempting to stand, but her ankle wasn't cooperating.

John took his hand away from his mouth. It was bloody, but he didn't make a move forward.

He pushed his tongue into his lip. "You ask her, Oliver. It's not my fault you brought a tart for a date."

Oliver went for another shot, but Morgan hooked

his leg with her arm. "Don't. He's not worth it. Please, let's just go."

Oliver stared down the other man for a moment before turning back to her. "You okay?" He lifted her to her feet, but she winced and nearly fell again when she put weight on her foot.

Oliver wrapped his arm around her to steady her. "He hurt you?" His anger made his words come out a growl.

She didn't want Oliver to fight. She just wanted to leave. "No, I tripped and twisted my ankle. Come on." She tugged him toward the door while leaning her weight on him.

"See, not my fault," John said, plastering himself against the wall.

Oliver pointed a straight, strong finger at him. "I'd keep my mouth shut if I were you." Then he turned and scooped up Morgan, carrying her out the door.

He walked confidently past the party without a second look and headed for the elevator, focused on the exit.

Their mode of departure drew the attention of the crowd, and Morgan cowered as people watched her being carried out.

"Oli, this isn't necessary," she whispered when they reached the elevator. "I can manage."

He didn't hear her. All he could think about was getting her out of there.

They entered the elevator, and he didn't make a move to put her down, but Morgan wasn't prepared to be carried around anymore, especially in such a small space. "Oliver. I'm serious. Put me down."

He continued to hold her tightly while Morgan struggled with him. "Oliver." She slapped his chest.

He looked at her. Their faces were so close they both stopped breathing. Morgan's eyes dropped to his lips, then she looked away. "I can walk. You can put me down."

He set her gently to the floor as the doors opened, and she held on to his shoulder while testing her ankle. It took a few tentative steps, but she was able to walk with a heavy limp into the lobby. She stopped and turned to him when he didn't follow.

His head sagged. "I'm sorry."

"For what?"

"For what John did. It's my fault."

Morgan sighed. "It's not your fault."

"It is. I was supposed to be watching him."

"True," she said with a grin in an attempt to lighten the mood. "What happened there?"

"Gillian caused a scene."

"Don't tell me she jumped out of another cake."

Oliver allowed himself to laugh. "No, she pretend fainted on me and I lost sight of John." The smile was gone in an instant. "I'll never put you in harm's way again."

Morgan couldn't take the intensity of his gaze. "Oh, don't be so dramatic. I'm fine. I'm just a little shaken. And besides, it was worth it, 'cause I got my virus uploaded. What do you think Raquel will say?" She winked.

Oliver remained solemn. "I should have just told her what we were looking for. She would have let us in. We didn't need to do it that way."

"Oliver, seriously. You can't be held responsible for everything that goes wrong. Now, let's go so I can get some ice on my ankle." She hobbled back to him and lifted his hand. "And it looks like you might need something for your hand."

"It's been a long time since I've hit anyone."

She ran a thumb across his grazed knuckles, and her face crumpled into a frown. "No one has ever defended me like that before."

"I've wanted to hit him for a long time. You did me a favor."

"That's not what I mean. No one's ever cared enough before."

She was still holding his hand, and he twisted it, his hand enveloping hers.

The moment stretched as her pulse hammered under his fingers. He had never wanted to kiss anyone so much in his life.

His lips parted, but he'd lost control enough for one night. "Wait here. I'll get Peter to bring the car around."

He left her staring out the door after him. She had no idea what had just happened, but he obviously hadn't felt what she had. She took a deep breath to reset herself but couldn't settle the pounding in her chest.

Chapter 19

BACK AT HOME, Oliver brought Morgan into his apartment to get the ice. He hadn't touched her again, and Peter's presence in the car had had a calming effect that brought her back to her senses and reminded her that this was a business arrangement, not a romantic one.

She looked around the room that was almost identical in setup to her side, but a baby grand piano sat near the window, close to where the computer was in her room.

Morgan limped over to it and sat on the bench. She ran her fingers along the keys.

"You play?" Oliver asked as he piled ice into a towel.

Morgan positioned her fingers and began "Moonlight Sonata." After playing for a minute, she stopped.

"Keep going. That was great."

"That's all I know." She sighed and her fingers slipped back into her lap. "I had a friend who played.

She taught me that much. Do you play? Or is this just decoration?"

"I play a little, but I have the piano for my mom. She's classically trained and I love to listen to her when she visits."

Morgan smiled down at the keys. "That's nice. Does she visit often?"

"Not very. She lives in France."

"Oh, really? Why France?"

"It's where she grew up."

"And your dad? Is he in France too?"

"He passed away a few years ago. Left me the business."

"Oh, I'm sorry to hear that."

Oliver shrugged. "We weren't that close."

"Just close enough to leave you his business." Oliver shrugged again but didn't respond. She twisted around on the seat to face him. "Wright and Lavigne. You're Wright, who's Lavigne?"

"That's my mom's maiden name. You ready for some ice?" he said, lifting the pouch he'd made.

"Maybe I should get on to Potters and find the link we're looking for."

"No, it can wait till morning."

"If you're sure." She hobbled back to the couch and rested her foot on the coffee table. "Thanks for this. It doesn't look too swollen, but it's very sore."

"The ice will help," Oliver said as he lowered it, positioning it so it covered the injured area. "You remember the first time we met?" he said as he went back to the kitchen for his own bag of ice.

"Define *met.*"

"The first time you served me." He sat down in a nearby chair, pushing his fist into the ice.

"Hmm. Not sure," she lied.

"I said I had lost my appetite."

"Oh, yes. Now I remember."

"I don't know why, but that's eaten away at me."

"I was interrupting you. I get it."

"That's what I was afraid you thought. It wasn't directed at you. I had just gotten some terrible news, and you saw my reaction to it."

She laughed. "Is that what happened?" She settled back into the couch. "Camilla was right. I was so offended ... But then I guess I wanted to be."

"Why would you want to be offended?"

"It's stupid."

"I'm sure it is." Oliver leaned forward. "But I still want to know."

"Camilla was pushing me on you."

"Really? Why?"

"I don't know. I guess she thinks you're hot stuff." She lifted a shoulder, trivializing it.

"And you obviously disagree."

"Well, honestly, I just wanted to be left alone. Not to mention that you have a man bun." Her face puckered.

"A what?"

"You know, when you tie your hair back. A man bun."

Oliver ran his hand through his hair. "Sometimes I need to keep it out of my face."

"You could get it cut."

"But I like it this length."

She sighed. "I guess it does suit you."

"So I'm forgiven?"

"For that."

"Oh, so there's more? Don't tell me, you don't like the way I ... drive my car?"

"No, the car's okay. But you know what's really offensive?"

"Do I want to know?"

"Yeah. This view you have here. It's pretty horrendous."

"Oh that. Yeah. I've tried to fix it, sent out thousands of letters asking people to turn their lights off at night so I don't have to look at all of that, but they won't listen."

"Losers."

"Yeah."

After a silent moment, Morgan said, "Hey, on a serious note. Can I ask you something? When you lost your appetite, what was that all about? You don't have to tell me, but I was just wondering."

He rubbed his hand across his mouth. "I made the wrong choice and people got hurt. I thought it was right, but I was wrong."

"But you made the best choice you could?"

"I thought I did."

"So what's the problem?"

Oliver sighed. She already knew he was a Christian, so he may as well be honest. "Not that you'd understand, but I prayed about it. A lot. I thought it was what God wanted."

"So he tricked you?"

"He didn't trick me. I just heard him wrong."

"So he tricked you."

"No, like I said, I made a mistake."

"But you say you asked him, and you felt you heard an answer. You made your choice based on that. If God made you *feel* right about it, but it was wrong, then he tricked you."

"My concern lies more around the fact that I heard him incorrectly. That I misunderstood his voice. All along I've thought he and I had a pretty good relationship, but maybe I've been wrong. Maybe I can't hear his voice as well as I thought I could."

"So you … have conversations with God. Like, *the* God. You two are friends?"

"Yeah, well, it's more than that, but sure, that's part of it."

"Interesting." Morgan drummed her fingers on the arm of the couch. "If Miss Richardson were here, what would she say?"

"Who?"

"My Sunday school teacher. She would say that God is a loving God who sent his son to die for me and my sins, and I need to ask him into my heart so I can be forgiven for my sins and apparently be friends with him."

"Yeah, that's a pretty good Sunday school sum-up."

"You've already done the asking him into your heart part, so if he's really the loving God that Miss Richardson says he is, wouldn't he have made it clear if you'd chosen wrong even if you heard him wrong in the first place? I mean, you said people's lives were at stake, so we're not talking about asking him what color tie you should wear for the day."

"True."

"So if he's not trying to trick you, and we're also assuming that you were indeed listening properly and not just wanting a certain answer so not really listening in the first place, right?"

"How do you even know to ask that question?"

"I've done it before. I mean, not with God, but with people trying to give me good advice and I only hear what I want to hear. So you didn't do that, right?"

He thought for a moment. "Right."

"And if he's supposed to be all-powerful, isn't it possible for him to let you know before it's too late? Or at the very least fix your mistakes, or make something good come out of it? I mean, we are talking about the supposed creator of the universe here."

"I can't believe I'm being preached to by someone who doesn't even believe in the God she's supporting."

Morgan shrugged. "I like to keep an open mind on all sorts of issues."

"Sounds very noncommittal."

"This coming from a man who's double minded about the God he serves." She laughed, not realizing what a slap in the face that was for him.

Oliver pressed his lips together. *I'm hearing you*, he said up to heaven.

Morgan checked her ankle. "I don't know why you're getting so caught up in it anyway. You've got so much, it's like you're looking for a reason to make life difficult. Even with that thing back at the party. You were trying to take full responsibility. It's like you want life to be painful for you. Trust me when I say, it's not a nice place to be."

"Well, trust me when I say, I've been through plenty of difficulties. It's the last thing I want to add to my life, but I won't shrug off my responsibilities simply because I don't want life to be hard."

"*You've* had plenty of difficulties." The weariness and fear from the evening, along with the confusion over her feelings for Oliver and the way he pushed her away, descended on Morgan in a wave.

"I've had more than my fair share."

"What, like, difficult decisions to make in your multi-million-dollar business? Or calling your private security firm to protect you so you can go play the big hero? I mean, have you ever even known what it is to struggle to survive? To not know where your next meal is going to come from? To have people abuse you simply because you're an easy target?"

"Would you believe me if I said I did?"

"Probably not. You say you know what it's like, but how can you? You've had everything handed to you on a silver platter. How can you know what it's like?"

Oliver suddenly looked a million miles away, and Morgan regretted attacking him. She couldn't even fully understand why she did it. "I'm sorry. I'm tired. I should go to bed. It's been a big night."

Oliver nodded. "Do you need help getting to your room?"

Morgan stood. "No, I'll manage. Good night."

Oliver didn't move from his chair. He sat staring at the door between their apartments, his mind spiraling.

Maybe it was better to leave a rift. It was certainly safer that way.

Safer for who and to what end?

He had already proven earlier tonight that he was coming close to not being able to trust himself around her, but if she was angry with him, then there was no risk. It still hurt, but it was an easier hurt to live with than the alternative.

Chapter 20

WHEN MORGAN WOKE UP, she lay completely still in her bed, remembering her words from the night before. It had been such a roller coaster of a night, but sitting and talking with Oliver was the first time in a long time that she felt at home. So why attack him?

Her skin crawled as she reran the last scene from the previous evening, so she got out of bed, still limping, and had a quick shower, washing it off as best as she could, before planting herself in front of the computer. The only place she felt truly in control.

There was a knock at the door and Morgan closed her eyes to brace herself for the awkwardness that was about to ensue.

"Come in."

"Hey, Morgan," Peter said, poking his head through the door.

"Oh, Peter. I thought you'd be Oliver."

"He asked me to check in on you. He had to go into work early."

Of course he did. "Shouldn't you be with him?"

"Liam's with him."

Morgan studied the computer screen. "I'm just getting to work on Potters' system."

"You guys were very quiet in the car on the ride home."

"It was a big night."

"Yeah, Oliver filled me in this morning."

Morgan's head drooped. "Did he tell you everything?"

"I don't know. He was very thorough, but I wouldn't put it past him to leave something out if he felt it was necessary. He did seem subdued."

"So he probably didn't tell you about how I attacked him last night." She didn't know what was compelling her to confess to Peter, but there was something about him that made her want to get it off her chest.

"*You* attacked him? No, he told me about John, but he didn't share that part."

"Not physically. I was just feeling insecure or something."

"Yeah, insecurity will do that to a person."

"It's just … He has *so* much." She waved a hand around the room. "And I was getting frustrated because he always carries all the problems of the world on his own shoulders. He takes responsibility for everything and it drives me crazy. He's had it so easy in life compared to so many others. He should just stop getting wound up about everything. I mean, he can't save the world."

"You've nailed him down quick. He does have a

tendency to carry too many burdens, and man is not made to carry those."

"You tell him that?"

"All the time."

"I just wish he'd enjoy the privilege that he has."

"You don't want him to suffer like you've suffered."

"I don't want him to *try* to suffer like I have."

"So I take it he hasn't told you? About his past?"

Morgan groaned. "No, don't say that to me." She leaned back, sliding down in the chair. "I was so afraid you'd say something like that." She plastered a hand on either side of her face as though she could protect herself from the truth. "That's the thing I've been dreading the most." She scooted back up and leaned forward, letting her head sag between her shoulders. "He said he knew what hardship was, and I said I didn't believe him. I'm such a jerk."

"All I can say is — that man is more complex than you know. There are some people you can safely draw conclusions about, but Oliver Wright is definitely not one of them."

"I've screwed up."

"You're human."

"But he'll never forgive me."

"Oh-ho." Peter laughed. "I've known Oli a long time and I can tell you in all certainty that he's already forgiven you. If he thinks there's anything to forgive."

She shook her head. "There is one thing I've come to hate more than anything, and that's when people assume things about me that aren't true. And look what I've just gone and done."

"Look at it this way. You've learned something valuable."

"Have I?"

"Sure. Next time someone assumes something about you, you'll go a little easier on them."

"I don't know that the lesson is worth the consequences."

Peter stood and patted Morgan on the shoulder. "I can tell you from a lifetime of experience that it usually is. Even if it doesn't feel like it, you'll likely change your mind later on."

"I hope you're right because I don't think I've ever felt worse in my life."

"Oh, come on. Now you're exaggerating."

His playfulness was a welcome relief. "You're right, I am. Thanks for listening and for being honest. I'm not used to getting that."

"Anytime. I'll check in on you a bit later, okay?"

Morgan picked at her fingernails for a few minutes after Peter left. She may have screwed up, but she could still help Oliver. She wasn't convinced that he'd have already forgiven her like Peter said, but she wanted to show him that she did care. Maybe someday she'd find a way to say sorry, but for right now, it was time to get her hands on the hard evidence she needed from Potters.

She had been sifting through the data for hours when

she finally found the email she had been searching for, and her spark returned.

When there was another knock at the door not long after, she was glad to be able to share her progress with Peter. "Yeah, come in."

Her confidence took a nosedive when she turned to see Oliver enter.

He offered a pained smile as he walked over. "How're you getting along?"

Morgan opened her mouth and then closed it, uncertain if she should apologize or keep the conversation formal. She took the easy way out. "I found it."

Oliver straightened at the news and hurried over.

She paused awkwardly for a moment, wanting to apologize again, but the fact that there was no malice in his countenance threw her off balance, and she couldn't find a way forward down that track so she dodged by showing him the email on the screen.

He read it through before speaking. "Vince Williams. I don't think I've ever heard that name at Potters."

"I looked him up. He's in accounting, but the weird thing is, he never opened the email."

"You can tell that?"

"Yeah."

"Maybe it went to his junk mail?"

"No, he got it in his inbox and then forwarded it to another address."

"Without opening it. So Vince is a middleman. Do you know where he sent it?"

"Overseas. I started following it just before you got here. Someone has worked hard to hide it."

"Can you follow it?"

"I should be able to. I'm in the middle of it now, so I don't have much else to say yet."

"Oh, I'm interrupting." Oliver jumped up and headed for the door. "I'll leave you to it then."

Morgan opened her mouth to stop him but still couldn't bring herself to voice an apology. Her words were useless to match what she needed to convey, so she let him go.

———————

Oliver paced his room. Peter had told him about the conversation he'd had with Morgan, but he wanted to wait until she brought it up. If she ever did. He'd expected her to jump straight onto it, so when she avoided talking about it, maybe it meant she'd let it drop. Not that it mattered. Except that when it came to Morgan, he was feeling more and more conflicted. He dropped into the closest chair and pressed his fingers into his eyes.

"God, I feel like I'm being torn apart." He was no stranger to pressure, but after what happened with the boat, and then having his life threatened — adding Morgan to the mix was making it harder than ever to see the right way forward. "If I'm on the wrong track somewhere here, can you please tell me?"

Keep moving. I've laid out the path. Just walk on it.

Oliver scrubbed his hands over his face. He hated when God said things like that, but he didn't have time to mull it over because his phone vibrated in his pocket.

It was a text from Morgan saying she'd found the end of the line. He blew a breath up at the ceiling, then lifted himself out of the chair.

"I almost lost it," she said, pointing to a line of code.

Oliver pulled his chair closer to the screen and narrowed his eyes. "I don't know what that means."

"Squinting doesn't make it clearer. Trust me." They shared a grin that turned clumsy, and Morgan jerked her attention back to the screen. She cleared her throat. "They almost sent me on a wild goose chase. But in the end" — she highlighted a line with the cursor — "this is the email address. It originates in Libya. I'm trying to figure out who it belongs to, but so far I've only been able to narrow it down to a region."

Oliver pulled out his phone and began typing. "I may be able to help. I've got connections over there and Peter has a few as well. If it's connected to me, there's a good chance something will pop."

"Okay, good. In the meantime, I'll keep looking."

"Great. You want me to leave you to keep working then?" He stood to leave.

"No, wait." Morgan bit her fingernail, then licked her lips to buy her a second. "Listen. About last night."

"Hey, don't worry about it. It was a rough night. I hope your ankle is feeling better, by the way. I forgot to ask."

"It's better, yeah. A bit stiff this morning but —

never mind that. What I said last night. I'm sorry. I didn't know about your past. Not that it should matter."

Oliver put his hands on his hips. "Peter told me he mentioned it."

"I hope you're not mad at him for saying something."

"I've learned to trust Peter's instincts on this stuff."

"Good. He, um … He told me I shouldn't assume things about you, and he's right. Most of what I said, I didn't mean anyway. Even without knowing anything else about you."

"Most?"

"We both know there's always truth when you lash out at someone. I won't insult you by denying that."

Oliver sat back down in the chair.

Morgan shifted uncomfortably in her own. "But I wish you said something last night."

"Like what?"

"I don't know. You could have told me I was wrong? Put me in my place?"

"And what would that have accomplished?"

Her shoulders dropped. "I would have felt less bad this morning."

"You don't need to feel bad. I told you it's fine."

"No, it's not. I was unfair. I do wish you would have told me last night, though."

"It's not a nice story and it had been a big day."

She twisted her fingers around one another. "Would you tell me anyway?" She quickly added, "It's okay if you don't want to."

"It's not that I don't want to." He scrubbed a hand

down his face and his eyes traveled to the window, unfocused. "You sure you want to know?"

"I really do."

He took a moment to collect his thoughts. "When I was eleven, my family moved to Venezuela. My dad had a growing business and there were new opportunities opening up over there that he was positioned to take full advantage of. But it was a risky move." He looked back at her, bracing for her reaction. "A lot of kids from rich families were being taken for ransom."

Morgan's eyes widened. "No. You?"

"My dad was already wealthy, but his profits were growing enormously at that time."

"What about protection? Didn't you have any security?"

"Yeah, he had hired security for me, but that's not really helpful when the man you hire takes a bribe." Morgan put a hand to her mouth but didn't speak. "The group that took me had a reputation for sending kids back in pieces whether they got paid or not, and my dad was a very stubborn and proud man. I died to him the day I was taken. He never expected to see me again, so when they asked for a ransom, he refused."

Morgan closed her eyes. "But they didn't kill you."

"No. And to this day, I have no reasonable explanation for it. They kept me at a camp in the middle of the jungle. I spent most of my time locked up in a small box. I honestly don't know how I didn't die in that box. It was sweltering and hard to breathe. Every time they threw me back inside, I had to focus on keeping calm. Keep my breathing steady and slow, which wasn't easy because most days they'd take me out and beat me up."

Morgan shook her head. "I don't … That's horrifying."

"Yeah." He reached a hand across his chest and rubbed his shoulder without realizing.

"Is that when you hurt your shoulder?"

He looked down at it and nodded. "One day they were throwing me around and my arm popped out of its socket." Morgan gasped. "When it happens once, it's never the same."

"Did they do anything about it?"

"Oh sure. They had someone who acted as a doctor for them. He put it back in, but that became the new thing they did, pulling my arm out."

"I don't understand how you've gotten your life back together after that. I can't even believe you survived."

His mouth twisted. "I wanted to kill myself. I almost did a couple of times, but something always stopped me. Then one night when they shoved me back in my box, the latch didn't close properly. I waited until the camp went quiet and I escaped."

"Just like that? How long had you been there?"

"About three weeks."

"And you survived the jungle?"

He shook his head. "I didn't expect to. That wasn't even why I escaped. I had no expectation that I'd survive. As soon as I got away from the camp, I found a spot under a tree and sat down to die. All I wanted at that point was to die free and unafraid, not stuck in a box as a slave." An odd smile lifted one side of his mouth. "I felt so at peace when I sat down. So relieved to die free."

"But you didn't."

"No. I don't know how long I sat there, but I heard something crashing through the jungle, and I was terrified it was my captors looking for me, so I got up and ran. I'm sure it was just an animal, but the thought of going back there was not something I could face."

"I can't believe I said all those things to you last night. Here I was thinking I had it bad. But listening to you, I mean … I don't think I would have survived."

"But that's the thing. I shouldn't have survived. I wandered around in the jungle for … days, maybe? I don't even know. I just knew I was injured and hungry and had no way of getting food. But I kept wandering around. Maybe it was because I wanted to get as far away from the camp as possible, but I could have been going around in circles for all I knew."

"So what happened?"

"I came across a sharp stick lying in the path I was walking."

"A stick saved you?"

"In a way." He shook his head. "I could barely hold it, I was so weak. It was useless. I knew it was, but in my growing delirium, I must have thought I could use it as a weapon or something. But I was so weak, it wasn't long before I sat down, ready to give up." Oliver frowned and looked out the window.

Morgan scooted forward on her chair. "And?"

"This next part you may find hard to believe."

Chapter 21

OLIVER SHOVED his hands in his pocket, unsure how to move forward with the story.

Morgan squirmed in her seat. She wanted to give him the space to tell his story, but the pressure became unbearable. "So, are you going to tell me?"

"I heard a voice." He watched her fight against her reaction. "Not out loud. Sort of in my head."

"You mean like how you have conversations with God?"

"Kind of, but louder."

"But you were delirious. Could it have just been that?"

"Sure."

"But you don't believe it was."

"No."

"Why?"

"Because of the next part. The voice insisted that I was going to live and that I needed to get up. I remember batting at the air as if I could push the thought away because I was so tired, and I wanted to lie down and die. But it came again. Louder, if that's even possible. So I stood. And when I did, I saw a pig down in a ravine."

"Don't tell me this is where the sharp stick came into play."

He smiled. "I looked at my pitiful spear, knowing full well that it was useless." He shrugged. "But I threw it anyway. I think my intention was to shut up the voice in my head." He took a step closer to her. "But I kid you not, that stick went into the pig and the pig dropped dead on the spot." Morgan raised her eyebrows. "I told you it was hard to believe."

"You sure you didn't imagine it?"

"You don't forget the taste of raw pig."

Morgan made a face and gagged. "No, now, that's just not right." She pressed her hand over her mouth.

Oliver laughed, the weight on his chest easing. "I was desperate. And that was another miracle — that I didn't get sick. But I did gain strength. It gave me the energy I needed to keep going until I found a small village that turned out to be close by. They looked after me for a couple of days while I recovered, and then they brought me into town."

"After all the grief I gave you last night, you never once hinted that you had that in your past."

"I didn't want to diminish your pain. What you've been through isn't nothing. It's very significant to your life."

"Your parents must have been so overwhelmed seeing you."

"Yes and no. My mom never forgave my dad for not paying the ransom. I think when I turned up she felt even more justified in her anger."

"That would have been tough. So I take it they didn't stay together?"

"Oh, no. They stayed together. My mom is a strict Catholic and would never divorce him, but I watched the bitterness eat her alive from the inside out."

"I thought you said she was still alive?"

His lips pressed together in a thin line, and his eyes dropped to the floor. "She is, but the light went out of her. That's why I have the piano, because she still plays, and when she does, I see a little spark come back. But she's never forgiven my father. Even after his death, she wears her malice like a protective cloak, as if it will stop more bad things from happening, not realizing that the most destructive thing in her life she's doing to herself."

"I can't say I blame her, though. So what happened to you after that? I can't imagine you could just go back to life as it was."

"No. The first thing my dad did was get me private lessons in fighting and survival. It was actually really good. It gave me more confidence in myself, and I became a very skilled fighter which has come in handy a few times, but the unexplainable part of my survival was always itching at the back of my mind."

"So you weren't a Christian before then?"

"My mom had always taken me to mass, so I knew what religion was, but I didn't really know God. Not the idea of him being a God that actually cared about me and spoke to me. My picture of him was always that he was far away. Too important to bother with me. Probably a bit like my dad. But after what happened, I talked to the priest about it. You should have seen his face. He suggested I was hallucinating."

"You have to admit, it makes sense. I mean, not you killing the pig, but the other stuff can be explained away."

"Yeah, it would have been a convenient way to sweep the hard stuff under the carpet. It would have been easier for sure, but I wasn't satisfied with that.

"I had nightmares for a long time. It was horrible, but the one thing those dreams kept reinforcing was that I shouldn't be alive. There was a reason that I was alive and I wanted to know why, so I decided to have a look for myself."

"Man, where do you start looking for those kinds of answers?"

"The Bible. I wanted to see what it had to say. Then God brought people into my life after that who helped me understand. But it was the Bible that introduced me to Jesus. I came to the conclusion he was with me in the jungle and he was the one that saved my life. For a reason."

"Ah, I see. And you've been trying to save the world ever since."

"Well, no. I may have figured out it was God, but I didn't really understand what that meant, and I still had a lot of baggage to deal with."

"No kidding."

"We moved to America after that, and I had a lot of

unresolved fear and anger to deal with. I went off the rails in my teens and into my early twenties."

"Don't we all."

"Fell in love with women and very expensive alcohol."

"Ah yes, that's right. The pricy liquor. And the ladies too? You were in love?"

"Not that kind of love. I was in love with the idea of women. I was never with one long enough to actually fall in love."

"Wow. So where was God in all of this? He went through all that trouble to save you and then you ignored him? You think he was mad?"

"I think he was sad, and I think it hurt him a lot when I shoved him into a box — just like I had been." Oliver swallowed the lump.

"Ouch."

"Yeah. But he was very, very patient as well."

"Okay, so what happened that finally changed everything for you?"

"One of the girls I was dating killed herself. That was my big wake-up call. That's when everything changed for me."

"One of the girls?"

"Yeah. I was not a nice person at that time in my life."

"Right. Well, that is quite a story."

"Now you know pretty much all of it. All my dirty laundry."

"I'm glad you told me. It's a hard story to hear, but I

think I understand you a little better now. And you were right, you know."

"About what?"

"I just thought you deserved to know after opening up to me. My roommate who framed me. I was in love with him, and he used that against me."

Oliver nodded. "Love can be a very dangerous thing."

Morgan slipped her hands between her knees. "I guess if I had God do something miraculous for me in my life, I might believe in him too."

"I think you'd be surprised if you went looking."

"If I go looking, what I find is bad stuff."

"But I had bad stuff too. I just allowed God to use it to make me a better person — eventually."

"You never blamed him for it?"

"Oh, you mean the 'Why does bad stuff happen to good people?' argument."

"Yeah."

"I have an answer for that."

"Do you?"

"Yeah, but I not going to tell you."

"Why not?"

"Because right now, you're looking for every reason to reject God. There's nothing I can say to convince you otherwise. But I'd encourage you to go to him and ask for yourself. If you're brave enough."

She wouldn't take the bait. "Now you're proselytizing. You know, there was a woman at the prison who tried to convert everyone. She had this silly grin on her face all the time. It put people off."

"She had freedom. I imagine in a prison, that's frowned upon. How can you have freedom when you're locked up? But choosing to become a Christian isn't always easy. I mean, it does require something of you."

"Miss Richardson said it was free."

"Oh, it's free all right. It's one of those things that costs you nothing and everything all at the same time. But I know from personal experience that it isn't easy to hand over control of your life. It wasn't until I realized that the control I thought I had was an illusion that I finally stopped resisting."

Oliver's phone rang.

"Saved by the bell," Morgan muttered. Their conversation was going in a direction she wasn't prepared for.

"It's Peter." Oliver put it on speaker. "Hey, Peter, what have you found?"

"The owner of the email. Oliver … It's Aaban Faraj."

Oliver lifted his face to the ceiling. His expression tightened in a fight for restraint. "Of course it is. I should have guessed."

"Who's Aaban Faraj?" Morgan asked.

"He's someone Peter and I have history with and he's recently resurfaced. I've been working in the background to try and stop him. That boat that sank, that was part of my efforts." Oliver lifted the phone closer to his face. "Peter, that means he's now working with people inside my company."

"Yeah. Liam's given me his thoughts, but we don't have any solid leads yet."

Oliver's phone had another call come through. "Peter, I'll call you back. Arthur is calling." He hung up and took the call. "Arthur, what can I do for you?"

"I'm glad I got through to you. There's been a development."

"By the tone of your voice, I'm guessing it's not a good one?"

"It's Faraj. I've gotten word he's planning something big."

Oliver closed his eyes. His jaw flexed. "I wonder if it's why he tried to kill me. He must have found out I was on to him."

"What?"

"Yeah, we just found out he's involved with the assassination attempt."

"I told you it was coming from the outside ... Well, maybe that's a good thing."

"How's that?"

"We can solve two problems. If we get over there quickly, we can organize protection for the village and maybe get a chance to take out Faraj once and for all. Solves both your problems. Peter's still set up over there, right?"

"Yeah, he's been coming and going, mostly consultant work these days ... but I didn't want to go back in there. We were both trying to keep our distance."

"I don't think we have a choice. They haven't been able to mobilize anything after what happened with the boat."

"I'm sorry you've gotten caught up in all of this."

"Are you kidding? This is the stuff I live for. Besides, I'm invested in this. I want to help."

"All right. You're right. We're going to have to go over."

"I'm coming," Morgan added before the conversation could go any further. "I don't know what their computers are like over there, but I can help."

"No way," Oliver said.

"I think she's right," Arthur said.

"We're not bringing Morgan. She's already been in enough danger."

Morgan's temper flared. "I think that's up to me to decide, isn't it?"

"Oli, we can keep her safe. Black's compound is secure. She'll be fine. She doesn't need to go out on the field. Morgan, do you have a passport?"

"I certainly do."

"Hang on," Oliver said. "Let me talk to Peter and see what he thinks. Then I'll get back to you."

He hung up the phone and looked at Morgan. "You're not coming."

"You said you were going to ask Peter."

"He'll agree with me."

"I'd like to hear that from him."

That seemed to satisfy Oliver. "Fine." He called Peter back and gave him the rundown.

"I think it's a good idea," Peter said, when Oliver mentioned Morgan. "She can remain in the compound. And she's right. She has valuable skills. I've got good guys over there, but not like her. There is a lot more going on online these days and if she can hack into that, it could give us a valuable lead."

"But it might not."

"Oliver, she'll be fine. It's too big a benefit to pass up. I'm sorry, but I think she should come. I'll leave it up to you guys though."

When Oliver hung up, Morgan threw her arms up in victory.

"You're gloating," Oliver said.

Chapter 22

MORGAN HAD BEEN on a plane once and only had a passport because she went with some friends on a trip to Mexico just before she was arrested. But being on Oliver's company jet was a completely different experience.

She stretched her legs out in front of her. "I'd be happy to stay on the plane the whole time," she said to Peter when he sat down across from her.

"Enjoy it while you can. The compound is not nearly as comfortable. By the way." He reached into his bag before he tucked it under his seat. "I have something for you." He lifted a necklace and dangled it in front of her. It had a long chain with a ball pendant swinging on the end.

"This is for me? Why?" She picked up the pendant and turned it around in her hands. Her finger caught on a small latch.

"It's from Jemi. I had her send it express the other night after I told you about her. She has these necklaces made up to give to people who support her work."

"What work?"

"She's still sending her scriptures all over the world. Mostly into places where the Bible is banned."

"She sends these?"

"No, they're too obvious. She still does the paper beads. These are just for people who don't have to hide anything. But she prays over each one and chooses a specific scripture, believing that the right one will go to the right person."

Morgan lifted the ball close to her face, admiring the intricate design. "She's prayed over this one?"

"Especially for you. When you open the latch, the ball unfolds and there is a scripture inside."

Morgan slipped the chain over her neck, afraid to open it. "That's very kind of her. Tell her thanks from me."

"I will, but really, I hope you'll be able to tell her yourself. We'd love for you to visit us at the farm sometime."

She laid the pendant carefully against her chest. "Why doesn't it surprise me that you have a farm? Where is it?"

"North Carolina. In the hills. You'd love it."

"I'm sure I would. Oliver ever been?"

"He's gotten out there once or twice, but it's hard to slow him down long enough most of the time."

Oliver and Arthur joined them after speaking to the captain. Oliver sat down beside Morgan and opened his laptop.

"I don't know how you can work at a time like this,"

Morgan said, rocking her head sideways to look at the screen.

He gave her a playful nudge away. "Not work for my company. I'm going over some of the reports from our last encounter with Faraj."

Peter leaned forward. "I've spoken to the guys on the ground. They're trying to get intel on his current location. If we're lucky, they'll have found something by the time we land."

"Unlikely." Arthur said, adjusting himself in the chair across from Oliver so he was comfortable. He clasped his hands over his stomach and closed his eyes.

"That's why I said we'd be lucky. But this stuff never depends on luck."

Morgan groaned. "You're not going to start talking about this Higher Power of yours again, are you? I should get out of your way."

"Sorry." Peter pointed at a red light on the ceiling. "Seat belt sign's not turned off. You're stuck."

"Just pretend you're sleeping," Arthur said with his eyes still closed. "That's what I do." He grinned.

Peter didn't bother pushing it and the plane settled into a comfortable silence filled in by the hum of the engines.

After trying and failing to take a nap, Morgan excused herself to the bathroom. She hadn't been able to take her mind off the pendant.

Once she had the safety of privacy, she flicked open the latch and the ball fanned apart. It surprised her to find her pulse increasing. She held her breath as she read the scripture written across the folds:

Death wrapped its ropes around me; the terrors of the grave overtook me…Then I called on the name of the LORD: "Please, LORD, save me!" (Psalm 116:3-4)

Morgan pulled in her chin. "That's weird," she said, folding the pendant closed. The necklace itself was beautiful, and the sentiment sweet, but there was no way Peter's wife had heard correctly from God. If there was one. Not that Morgan didn't appreciate the gesture, but Jemi got it wrong.

When she returned to her seat, she found Oliver typing on his computer. Peter was snoring, and Arthur looked like he was in a blissful state of meditation.

Oliver closed his laptop and put it away. "You should try to get some sleep."

"I don't know how they do it." She nodded toward Peter and Arthur. "I don't think I can sleep well on planes."

"Peter can sleep anywhere. I don't know whether he learned that out of necessity, or if he's just a natural. And Arthur's been on enough planes it wouldn't faze him."

"Listen, Oliver, I didn't want to ask before because there was so much going on. But what has this Faraj guy done?"

Oliver rubbed at his dry eyes. "He's head of a small terrorist group. It's the reason Peter and I started working together. They aren't big enough for the American government to worry about, but they're murdering people and stealing their children."

"Oh," Morgan whispered. "Hit's close to home."

"Years ago I went over there and tried to stop him myself — with Peter. I thought I had succeeded. Then last year, he popped up again. I tried to help them set up protection for themselves. I sent the ship across the Mediterranean. It was carrying medical supplies, but also a box of gems we were trying to smuggle. The gems were to go to a small team that was being assembled. It was to help fund their resistance. So when the boat sank, and I lost it, they had no way of hiring any help. Now it sounds like Faraj might be attempting to wipe them out. And the only reason I can think is out of spite."

"Why didn't you just send more money?"

"It's not as simple as that. The gems would have been untraceable and they were worth a lot."

"So how does us going over there now change things?"

"There are ways I can use my business to help coordinate everything, especially since we already have a relationship with a group there. But there are consequences to doing it that way. It will entail a lot of cleanup when we get back to the States, but I can't let Faraj wipe out all those people."

"Then I'm glad I've come. If I can help stop that, it's definitely worth it. I've never done anything this important before."

"Listen, Morgan ... I know I didn't want you to come originally, but I am glad you're here. You've already done so much, and I know you're a great addition to the team. I just hope it's enough to stop the massacre."

"I thought you didn't need hope if you had God."

"No, if we have hope in God, it's luck we don't need."

"Right. Sure. Well, I guess we should get some sleep."

The seat leaned back comfortably, but sleep continued to elude her as her mind raced. She felt over-whelmed by the complexities of the fight she now found herself in the middle of. This was a huge responsibility she didn't know if she was prepared for. Even the excitement of being a part of something important like this didn't outweigh the weight she now felt.

At the airport, Morgan kept her mouth shut as they dealt with the airport security and customs. She tried to stop looking at the giant guns everyone carried, but her eyes had a mind of their own.

Finally, they collected their luggage and moved to the awaiting SUV. Peter greeted the driver like they knew each other well, and Morgan jumped when he slapped the top of the vehicle to indicate it was time to depart.

"Bulletproof," Arthur said, turning back to Morgan from the front seat once they set off.

"What?"

He knocked a knuckle on the window. "They're bulletproof, the cars. You look nervous. I thought you might like to know."

"I'm okay. It's just new." Morgan found more

comfort in the press of Oliver's shoulder into hers than the build of the cars, as ridiculous as she knew that was.

She focused on the unusual monotony in the muted colors of the outside world as it sped by and tried to imagine what it would be like to live there. She looked at the faces of the people they passed and attempted to picture what their life was like. Or what it would be like to live in a village that a madman was about to destroy.

It was strange to think that Oliver, who had grown up with more money than he probably knew what to do with, had more idea of what life was like for these people than she did.

It was less than half an hour before they arrived at a large walled-off building. Two armed men opened the gate before they entered into the safety of the compound. Morgan noticed Oliver physically relax once the vehicle had passed through.

She bumped him with her elbow. "You're tense."

He looked at her, his face a solemn mask. "I feel responsible for you. I probably shouldn't, and you might not like it, but I do."

It was a strange comfort hearing him say that. It probably shouldn't be, but she couldn't deny it.

A woman in fatigues standing at attention greeted Morgan when she exited the SUV.

Peter shook the woman's hand. "Morgan, this is Rodriguez. She'll show you to your room."

Morgan was unhappy when she was separated from

the group, but had a suspicion there were things they didn't want her to know.

"So, Rodriguez. I take it that's your last name?" Morgan asked to fill the silence as they walked the maze of halls.

"Yes, ma'am."

"Anyone here have first names?"

Rodriguez smiled stiffly, but it wasn't absent of warmth. "Just you."

By the time they reached a large open room with bunk beds, Morgan had gotten turned around and had no idea where they were from where they had come.

"Pick whichever you like that's empty." Rodriguez went to a locker and put something in it before turning back to Morgan, who had dropped her bag on the closest bunk. "Is this your first time in Libya?"

"This is my first time anywhere outside of North America."

"It's unfortunate you won't get a chance to see the country."

"No. I didn't expect to. I don't think I'll get past the walls of this building if Oliver has anything to do with it."

"It's for your own protection."

"So I've been told."

"What's your area of expertise?"

"Computers."

Rodriguez nodded. "The bathroom is through there. Get yourself settled in and I'll be back to collect you later."

"Wait."

"Yes?"

"I'm just supposed to wait here?"

"Yes. Get some rest."

Morgan thanked her, then stood still in the middle of the room. She drummed her fingers on her leg. Her head was fuzzy after the flight and she was tempted to lie down for a few minutes as Rodriguez suggested, but she knew that would wreck her for the rest of the day and she didn't want to miss anything.

After brushing her teeth and washing her face, Morgan didn't have to wait long before Rodriquez returned. "Oh good, you're awake. They've asked me to bring you in for the briefing."

"Good." Morgan nodded.

After descending what felt like multiple floors in an old industrial elevator, the cage opened into a room with screens covering the walls and desks with computers filling the middle.

Even with some high-tech gear, it wasn't like in the movies. The florescent lights over-illuminated the room and some of the computers were old, but it was still impressive to be surrounded by the hive of activity.

Peter caught sight of Morgan's entrance, and he walked over to collect her. "How you feeling?"

"Moderately overwhelmed, but okay. Ready to help however I can."

"Good, because unfortunately, we don't have the luxury of time. Follow me."

He led her into a hospital-white conference room.

Oliver was up at the front, in front of a whiteboard still covered in marks from the last meeting. He was leaning over a desk, talking to another man.

"Have a seat over there." Peter pointed toward the back corner of the room and then went to join Oliver up front.

The two men spoke before Peter clapped his hands to get the attention of the room. "All right. Listen up. We've already dispatched a team to the village to give support and to be ready for any imminent attack. However, we have yet to establish confirmation that Faraj and his men are indeed on the verge of said attack, so at this point we are in information-gathering mode. We have with us Miss Caine." He motioned to the back where Morgan sat, and everyone turned. She shrank back and smiled nervously. Oliver put his thumb over his lips to hide his own smile at her reaction.

"She is the point man on any computer-related activities, and we are going to do everything in our power to get her inside enemy territory." Peter continued to walk everyone through the mission then he dismissed the group.

A heavyset man with glasses walked up to her and leaned over slightly to get her attention. "Caine?"

"Oh, hi. Yes. You can call me Morgan."

"Morgan. I'm Michaels."

"It's nice to meet you Michael."

"No, Michaels. Harvey Michaels."

"Oh, Harvey. I mean Michaels. Right. It's hard to get used to using last names all the time."

"Saves on the confusion." He laughed with his lips

puckered. "At least … I mean … you seem a bit confused."

"Yeah. This is sort of outside my normal."

"Civilian." Michaels nodded. "You get used to it. I'm computers too. I was top man on campus around here until you showed up." He pointed his fingers like a gun at her.

"Oh, I'm sorry. I never meant — "

"No, no. It was a joke. I'm not mad. I'm intrigued. I can't wait to see you in action." He blushed. "I'll be out there if you need me." He turned quickly and left.

Oliver saw she was free and approached. "How you holding up?"

"Fine. So should I be calling you Wright?"

Oliver smiled. "Call me whatever you like."

She perked up. "You mean that?"

"Within reason." He quickly added, "Do you need a break, or do you think you can have a look now? Everyone is eager to get started. We're already behind."

"Yeah, I can get started, assuming you have a place for me *to* look."

"We know where the email came from. What servers."

"Perfect."

Oliver set her up at a desk. "Anything you need, ask Michaels." He pointed to a desk a few feet away. Michaels saluted her, then got busy with work again when a red flush traveled up his neck.

"Where will you be?" she asked Oliver as he turned to go.

"Peter and I are going out with a team. We've got a few things to check out."

"Is that safe?"

"We've done it before."

"That's not what I asked."

"We'll be fine."

She nodded without responding further but watched as he walked away. She wanted to help, that's what she had signed up for. But what she hadn't anticipated was that the information she found could send Oliver into a dangerous situation. She saved his life once. She couldn't now turn around and do the opposite.

She stared at her computer screen, drumming her fingers on the keyboard. She'd just have to focus on finding the type of information that could stop this Faraj guy while keeping Oliver safe. If she found what they were looking for, maybe he wouldn't have to go back into the field.

Chapter 23

MORGAN CHECKED the time and rubbed her tired eyes. She had easily hacked into the system where the email came from, but so far, she had found nothing remotely interesting. And because nothing was in English, translating took time to complete before she could move onto the next thing.

She slid a paper clip off the desk and tapped it on her cheek. The words had started bleeding together, and she struggled to focus. She rubbed her eyes again, then laid her head down for a moment to rest them.

Oliver and Peter darted around the corner of the warehouse and took refuge behind several large crates. They had separated from the rest of the team when the targets they had been following separated.

"I spotted two armed guards on the door," Peter whispered.

"You think we have a chance of getting inside?"

"There's always a chance." Peter angled his head around a crate to get a second look. "If we come in from the side, we could take out those two, but we need to see who else is around first."

"Okay. You go left, I'll go right. We'll meet back here."

Oliver was pleased to find, as he scouted around his side, that there were no other guards to be found. That didn't mean there weren't any, but it was a good start, and when he arrived back at their meeting point at nearly the same time, they were both ready to attempt entry.

"What do you think Morgan will say when she hears about this," Peter said before they made their move.

"Why are you worried about what Morgan thinks?"

"I'm not worried, but I thought you might be."

"And why should I be worried?"

"This was never meant to be a risky mission. We only expected to follow the targets, not try to infiltrate their base."

"I'm here to save people's lives and that's what I'm doing."

"Okay, if you're sure."

"I'm sure."

"Then let's go."

The two men snuck around to the side before setting upon the two guards and taking them out, but before they could get the door open, there was a yell from outside the gate and two more men came running toward them with their weapons raised.

Oliver and Peter lifted their hands into the air. "Well, this is unfortunate," Oliver said.

"But not the first time. You ready?"

"Absolutely."

When Morgan regained consciousness, she stayed still, the weight of sleep hanging heavy on the back of her head. She should have expected to fall asleep. She was exhausted. Obviously, no one else was surprised enough to wake her either.

She lifted her head slowly and wiped the drool out of the corner of her mouth, her eyes darting to Michaels' desk to check if she'd been caught with spit on her face. But he wasn't there.

Her neck was tight, and she tipped it sideways, squeezing to release some tension as she scanned the room. It was nearly empty except for Arthur, who was sitting at another computer.

"Where is everyone?" she asked, her voice scratchy with sleep.

Arthur spun around. "Morgan, hey. You startled me." He swung back to turn his screen off. "I didn't realize you'd woken. Uh, I believe everyone else is getting a bite to eat. I thought I'd take the opportunity to get some paperwork done."

He smiled with his lips closed. Her eyes darted to the now blank screen of his computer. Oliver had done the same to her when they had met. Maybe it was her.

"Have Oliver and Peter come back yet?"

"Not yet, but we don't expect them back for a few more hours." He stood. "I'm going to get something to eat." He held out his hand for her to do the same. "You coming?"

Morgan stretched. "That sounds great. I'm starving."

The mess hall was on another floor and Arthur kept her entertained during dinner with stories of the various trips he'd done for Oliver. "Oliver and I are perfect for each other," he said. "I love to travel, and he loves sending me places."

"How long have you two known each other?"

"About four years, but he hired me to work for his company only last year. We had mutual contacts around the place. I had done a few things for him and he wanted to make sure I was compensated properly."

"Seems like putting your life on the line like this is going above and beyond."

"I don't mind. Keeps things interesting. I'm something of an adrenaline junkie."

Morgan's attention was drawn to the door when Oliver and Peter walked into the room looking haggard and dirty. Oliver's coat was torn, and he had a cut above his eye.

Morgan jumped from her chair. "What happened?"

"You going to tell her or should I?" Peter said, nodding his head her way.

"You go grab a bite to eat. I'll give her all the gory details."

"Rough night?" Arthur asked when Oliver pulled out a chair, the metal legs scraping on the floor.

"You could say that." Oliver fell into the chair with an "Oof." "We asked around in town. Some locals that we know. Got a lead, so we followed them to a warehouse, but when we tried to get in … well … let's just say things didn't go as planned."

Arthur chuckled. "I hate when things don't go as planned."

"Yeah."

"So I take it your life was in danger?"

"There was a moment or two. Jealous?" Oliver grinned, but it was half-hearted.

"Totally."

"Wait, is that true?" Morgan leaned forward. "Was your life really at risk?"

Oliver waved her question away. "We're fine. We were able to take the two guys out when they came to apprehend us."

Peter sat down with a full plate. "Your turn," he said to Oliver before levering a chunk of curried potato into his mouth.

Oliver hoisted himself out of the chair and went to get his own plate.

Morgan turned her attention to Peter. "How much danger were you two really in?"

Peter swallowed his food and breathed deeply. "Enough. I won't elaborate to my wife unless she makes me."

"Does she make you?"

"Usually, unless she's not in a good frame of mind to handle it."

Morgan sulked back into her chair.

"So, no luck?" Arthur asked.

"Nothing worth shouting about," Peter said with his mouth full.

Oliver came back and said nothing as the two men stuffed themselves. Arthur excused himself and Morgan wanted to but was unsure if she was allowed to go wandering around. She could feel her frustration bubbling away just under the surface, so she sat in silence with her arms folded, staring at the floor.

Peter scraped up his plate and looked at her. He sucked a bit of food out of his teeth, then looked at Oliver, who was focused on his food.

"I'm heading to bed," Peter said as he stood. Both Oliver and Morgan watched him return his dishes to the kitchen, then he left without saying a word to either of them.

Oliver finished his last bite and laid his silverware on the plate. He leaned back, full and satisfied. He was exhausted but energized from the outing, now that the danger had passed.

"How was the rest of your day?" he asked.

"Fine." She found she couldn't look him in the eye.

"You okay?"

"I'm fine." She scratched at a spot on the table with her fingernail.

"Is something bothering you?"

"I just didn't realize that saving your life was a waste of my time."

"Pardon me?"

"If you're going to go out and get yourself killed, then what was the point of me saving you in the first place?"

"Oh." He pushed his plate to the side and folded his arms, leaning them on the table. "I'm sorry you were worried. I didn't know it would bother you so much."

"It doesn't. I don't care. It's your life. Do whatever. I just didn't know I'd be wasting my time coming here." She still couldn't look at him.

"Listen, Morgan. I don't really understand why you're so mad."

"Why not? Peter's wife will be mad. Or at least very upset."

"But you're not my wife." Morgan's mouth snapped shut, and Oliver ran a hand through his hair. "Sorry, that came out wrong."

"No, I didn't — that's not what I mean. I just — never mind." Morgan spotted Rodriguez getting up from a nearby table. "Hey, Rodriguez, would you mind showing me where my room is again?"

"Morgan." Oliver reached out a hand toward her when she stood.

"Forget it. I'm sorry. I'm just overtired."

Oliver wasn't sure how to handle her response or even how he felt about it, so he let her go without saying another word.

Morgan woke up the next morning with a roaring headache. After having a nap at her computer the evening before, followed by the confrontation she had with Oliver — not to mention sleeping in a room with half a dozen other women who came in at different times during the night — it had taken her a while to fall asleep

She sat up in bed, wiping the sleep out of her eyes, then checked the other bunks. They were empty. She swung her legs over the side and leaned her elbows on her knees. Her head sagged between her shoulders.

She'd have to apologize to Oliver. Again. Her face heated when she recalled comparing her own response to Peter's wife's. But she couldn't deny the fact anymore that she felt something for Oliver. Whatever it was, she had tried to ignore it after the party incident, but it refused to budge. The fact of the matter was, she cared for him in a way that made her very uncomfortable, especially since he put her so absolutely in her place after the *wife* gaffe.

She had a shower to wash off her distress, and when there was still no one around, she decided she was going to have to find humanity in this rabbit warren on her own and hopefully not get too lost.

When she found the elevator, it occurred to her that she didn't know what floor the computers were on.

The elevator rattled, and she stepped back. Fortunately, when it opened, Rodriguez was on the other side.

"Oh, great. Morgan, I was just coming to see if you were awake. You want to head down?"

Morgan stepped into the elevator. "Thanks. Is everyone else up?"

"Yes, ma'am. Did you want breakfast first?" Her finger was poised over the buttons.

"No, I'm not hungry."

When she pushed the button, Morgan paid attention this time.

"Am I the last one up?"

"By several hours."

"Oh. So I'm late."

"Wright explicitly requested you be left to sleep as long as you needed."

"Of course he did." She wasn't sure if that was a good sign or a bad one.

When the doors opened, she scanned the room for Oliver, but he wasn't there. She made eye contact with Michaels, who smiled briefly, then went back to work.

"Guess I'll get busy." She looked for Peter and Arthur as she settled into her chair, but they weren't there either.

"Hey, Michaels."

His head shot up like a meerkat. "Yeah."

"Have you seen any of the guys that I came with?"

"Not since breakfast."

"Any idea where they are?"

"No, but they had an early briefing that I wasn't a part of."

"Thanks." Morgan's stomach tightened. They had another mission, and Oliver didn't want her worries getting in their way. She rested her elbow on the desk and drummed her fingers on her lip while she waited for the computer to log on.

She had to get over this crush. There were more important things at stake. There were other people's lives, and Oliver was out there trying to do good while she was in here only caring about her own feelings.

Once the computer had fired up, she rubbed her hands along her pants legs and set to work. But while she waited for the first translations to process, her eyes drifted sideways to the computer Arthur had been on yesterday when she woke up at her desk. She pinched her bottom lip in thought, but the rattle of the elevator drew her attention away.

A handful of people stepped off, including Oliver. They didn't look disheveled but were talking seriously and closely between themselves.

Oliver looked up from the huddle and spotted her, then headed her way. "Hey, I hope you had a good sleep."

"I wish you would have sent someone to get me up. I feel like I've wasted time."

"No, it's important you catch up on your rest while you can. You need to think clearly."

"So, about last night — "

He put a hand on her shoulder. "Morgan, please, don't even worry about it."

"I don't know why you find it so easy to put up with my outbursts. I seem to be making a habit out of it."

"And what makes me so lucky?" he joked.

"Perhaps the fact that I'm always exhausted around you." She didn't really like how that came out.

He held back a snicker and let it go. "Have you gotten online this morning?"

"Yeah, just started, but with all the waiting for translations and working through everything, it's been slow and I haven't really come up with anything. I'm sorry I haven't been more use. What about you? Have you guys been out again?" She kept her voice light and approving.

"We might have something, but it's too early to tell if it's a real lead. We've also just been to the village and they've reported that it's been quiet for them overnight, so that's good. Thankfully, we'll be able to put a few more guys out there soon, but we are really hoping to get on the front foot with this instead of simply taking a defensive position."

Morgan nodded

"I've got to keep moving," Oliver said, but paused to wait for her response.

Morgan clasped her hands in her lap and reminded herself that this was business, not personal. "Okay."

Oliver's head dipped in an uncertain nod, then he left.

After watching him go, her eyes wandered back to the desk Arthur had used. She tipped her head up to the ceiling and decided she'd find it easier to focus if she just checked on what he had been doing. If it was something confidential, she should be able to tell soon enough and then she could get back to work.

When she discovered her computer didn't have clearance to access the other computers, she perked up at the new challenge. A challenge she was confident she could overcome. And after meeting nothing but dead ends for the past day and a half, it was exactly what she needed to get her energy levels up.

She linked her fingers and cracked them before setting to work.

After retrieving the list of users, she found Arthur's name and searched for his login time from the previous night, but there wasn't one.

"Okay, let's see." Her tongue poked out the side of her mouth as she adjusted her search for the computer, instead of the user. It wasn't hard since there were only two of them logged on at that time.

A hand rested on her shoulder, and she jumped, swiveling around to see Arthur standing behind her. She resisted the urge to make the same mistake he had and shut the screen down. Right now it was filled with code and looked similar to other things she had been searching. It was safer to assume he had no idea what she was doing, rather than risk giving herself away.

"How are things going with you down here in the dungeon?" He glanced at the screen.

"Nothing yet. Still looking."

"What have you got there?"

"Oh, this? Just a list of times and dates of user access. I was looking at something yesterday that might be significant, but I can't remember where I found it. I'm looking back at my history."

"Not getting too bored?"

"No, I never get bored with this stuff. It's like a puzzle."

He patted her shoulder before removing his hand.

"Okay then, have fun with that. I'm more of a hands on kind of guy."

"Did you go out with them this morning?"

"Yeah. It was good to see everyone was safe over at the village."

"Good."

There was an awkward silence that neither one of them bothered filling. Finally, Arthur smiled, then left.

Morgan smiled back and then grimaced when he turned away. She waited until he was out of sight before she went back to the list.

After waiting a full minute to make sure he was definitely gone, she found the computer she was after. It was logged in with a different user name she didn't recognize and all that had been accessed was the email server.

She twisted around to confirm there was no one watching her and pulled up the email that Arthur had sent. It contained what looked like an address and there were photos attached. She brought up the photos. One was a picture of the front of the building they were in. Another looked like a loading dock.

She analyzed the email further in case there was something more that was hidden within the photos or text, but there was nothing else. She closed it down and leaned back in her chair.

Nothing about the email seemed sinister, but it was still odd.

"Hey, Michaels."

The meerkat again. "Yeah, what's up?"

"What's the address for this building?" He confirmed her suspicion that the address in the email was the building they were in. "Do people know what's in this building?"

"No way. This base is top secret. Cool, huh?"

Morgan's heart tumbled, and she jumped from her chair, knocking it over. "I need to find Oliver or Peter. Do you have any idea where they might be?"

"Whoa, what's wrong?"

An alarm sounded, and Morgan shrank back. "No no no no. Oliver. I need to find Oliver."

"It's okay. It's just an evacuation drill. They do these from time to time," Michaels said. "We go this way."

She followed him to a stairwell. "I really need to find Oliver."

"He'll be at the rendezvous point out the front."

The stomping of boots filled the stairwell, and Morgan heard her name from above. She spotted Oliver leaning over the railing. "Oli," she called up. "Something's wrong."

"I know. This is not a drill. Come on."

When they reached the landing, people were filtering out toward the front, but a door opened behind them. It was Arthur. "Oliver, Morgan, this way, quickly. I've got a car ready."

Morgan balked.

Oliver grabbed her hand and pulled her toward Arthur. "Come on, Morgan. We have to keep you safe."

Oliver dragged her through the door before she could stop him.

"Wait," she said, yanking back. "I think Arthur might be behind this."

"What?" Oliver looked down the hall, but Arthur had disappeared around the corner.

"Has he ever been here before?"

"No. This is his first time. Why?"

"Can we just go out the front with everybody else? Please. I'll be safe there too."

"Hey, it's okay. I organized the transport for us. Just in case something like this happened."

"Who came up with the idea?"

"What idea?"

"Having the car out the back. Was it your idea or Arthur's?"

"What difference does that make?"

"Oli, please. Can we just go out the front with everyone else? It will be safe."

Arthur appeared again. "You guys coming?"

"Just give us a sec," Oliver said, looking at Morgan's frightened face.

"We don't have a sec," Arthur said.

Morgan was scrambling. They couldn't go with Arthur. Not without an explanation. "I saw your email," she said to him. "And the pictures."

"Oh, that. I, um — " He tsked. "I guess it's better if I just show you." He put a hand in his coat and pulled out a gun.

Chapter 24

OLIVER LOOKED AT THE GUN, his expression remaining neutral. "What are you doing?"

"I really need you two to come with me."

"And if we don't?"

"Then I shoot you both."

"You're either a very good liar or I appreciated our friendship too much to see it coming."

"I am a pretty good liar." Arthur laughed.

"All this time. You were the absolute last person I suspected. I thought you believed in the good we were doing."

"Oliver, I want you to know that one of the hardest parts of this for me was knowing I'd lose your friendship. But when it comes down to it, I've got to do what's best for me. Besides, it's just good business."

"Whose?"

"Well, see, that was the problem. You were interfering with Faraj's business. He hired me to take you out of the picture in exchange for giving Wright and Lavigne profitable business for years to come."

Oliver scoffed. "You're telling me you did it to help my company?"

"Indirectly it gets me what I want, but we don't have time for this. Either come with me, or I just shoot the two of you. Works for me either way."

Oliver pushed Morgan behind him. "You don't need her. Just take me."

Morgan gripped the back of Oliver's shirt. She wanted to run, but not without him.

"Sorry, but because she interfered with the last plan, he's requested I bring both of you in. Let's go."

Oliver didn't move until Arthur lifted his gun. The look of indifference on his face convinced Oliver that he wouldn't hesitate to shoot. After stalling as long as he could, he twisted to put an arm around Morgan, keeping her close while Arthur led them at gunpoint out the back.

Morgan recognized the loading dock from the picture in Arthur's email. She entangled her fingers into the folds of Oliver's shirt to keep him close while they were loaded into the back of an old gray sedan with dark-tinted windows.

The man in the driver's seat kept his gun trained on the captives while Arthur moved into the passenger seat.

"Now, Oliver," Arthur said after pulling his door shut. "Can you do me a favor and don't try anything stupid? I'd rather not have to shoot you."

"Don't tell me you've found a modicum of conscience," Oliver said darkly.

"Conscience? No. But it would make a mess in here that I'd rather not have to clean up."

"When did you become so cold?"

Arthur shook his head as they approached the back gate. "I've always been cold and you know it. That's why I'm working for you, remember?"

There was a single guard there who Arthur saluted as they passed.

Oliver straightened, but seeing that Arthur didn't bother hiding his weapon, it was clear this guard wouldn't offer rescue, so he leaned back into his seat as they pulled on to the street.

"Now that we have time for a chat, can I ask what it is that you expect to get from all of this?" Oliver could feel Morgan trembling in the seat beside him. He reached across while he was speaking and put a hand over her fist. "You're not in line as my successor within the company."

"Oh no, I don't want to run your business." Arthur scrunched up his face. "I thought you knew me better than that. I simply want to be Wright and Lavigne's most valuable asset."

"How would that change anything?"

"Oliver, when we met, I was traveling around the world on a shoestring."

"I don't seem to recall you having any trouble getting what you wanted."

"I still don't." Arthur laughed. "I mean, come on, I even got what I wanted from you. You gave me a job because you thought you could make me a better man."

"I saw your potential, and I wanted to give you the

resources you needed to get the job done so you didn't have to steal them from someone else."

The side of Arthur's mouth curled. "And I appreciated those resources."

"I thought I was helping a friend."

"You were as much as a guy like me can have friends. You provided me not only with traveling comfort but also adventure. I didn't have to go begging for it anymore. And I always appreciated it. But you've kept me on too tight a leash over the years, and I want my freedom."

"I guess I'm a sucker."

"No, Oliver, you're a sap. Let me give you a piece of advice. This world?" He circled his gun around in a vague gesture. "It's not worth saving. You have to squeeze out of it what you can before you die."

"I'm sorry, but I'll never share your point of view."

Arthur smiled sadly. "I know. And ironically, that's what's going to kill you."

Oliver tried another angle. "They'll never go for it at Wright and Lavigne. They won't get into bed with a terrorist."

Arthur winced. "Terrorist is such a harsh term. Faraj is more of a businessman these days. And let's be honest, you're the only one there who ever cared. Everyone who sits at that table will happily look the other way to keep the shareholders happy. And me? I'll be able to make the terms that suit me. It's a win-win."

"Okay, so what about Morgan?" He felt her stiffen under his touch. "She has nothing to do with this. You have no reason to hold her."

Arthur tipped his head her way. "Sorry, it wasn't my call, sweetheart. Faraj wanted you in the bargain. Not that I'm disappointed. You made this entire process much more difficult. But I have to ask, what made you check my email? Was I that obvious?"

Oliver squeezed her hand tighter as she took a steadying breath before she spoke. "You turned off your screen. It stuck with me, and I couldn't let it go."

He huffed out a laugh and shook his head. "I can't say I'm going to be sorry to see the end of you. You've made me look bad, and I don't appreciate it."

Oliver wanted to take a swing at him but knew it would cause more trouble than it was worth, so he just kept a tight grip on Morgan's hand and they both went silent.

Watching out the window, he had a fair idea of the direction they were headed, which was a very bad sign. If there was a chance they would be released, blindfolds would have been used.

God, you need to get her out of this. I'm okay to die, but she's not. Please. His head dropped. *I knew I shouldn't have brought her. I may have screwed up, but please fix this for her.*

The car stopped in front of a gate that was pulled open by several armed men. Then they drove around the circle drive and stopped in front of an old building that looked like an abandoned hospital.

Another armed man approached Morgan's door, yanking it open while keeping his rifle trained on her.

Morgan slunk back against Oliver, but the man reached in and grabbed her arm.

"It's okay," Oliver whispered in her ear. "Just go with them. Resisting will make it worse."

After being pulled from the car, her shaking intensified, and she began hyperventilating.

Oliver leaned close as their hands were tied behind their backs. "Hey, slow your breathing. Everything will be okay. We'll be okay." He didn't like lying to her, but he didn't want her to pass out either.

Her head bobbed in a short sharp jab of acknowledgment before the guards shoved them forward, dragging them through a series of halls until they reached a wide arched door at the end of one.

When they entered, they found a broad, dark man in an expensive-looking suit sitting in a large armchair and reading the newspaper.

He flicked down the top of the newspaper to reveal a full beard that couldn't hide the deep scars in his face.

After folding the paper, he laid it on the table in front of him and stood. "Oliver Wright, how good of you to join us." He had a strong western influence to his accent.

"Aaban Faraj, are you trying to be clever?" Oliver shot back.

Faraj stepped around the table, smiling with closed lips. As he approached, his attention shifted to his other captive. "And you must be Morgan Caine."

Oliver pulled at his restraints. "She's got nothing to do with any of this. You have no reason to keep her."

Faraj stayed focused on Morgan, who had dropped her eyes to the floor. "We'll have to agree to disagree."

He put his fingers under her chin to lift her head, but she shook them off before looking him in the eye, attempting to show the same courage as Oliver.

He clasped his hands in front of him. "You're not what I expected," he said.

"I'm sorry to disappoint you."

She lifted her chin a fraction and Faraj smiled again, this time showing his straight, white teeth. "I don't usually like to be proven wrong, but this case is an exception."

He took a couple of slow steps to stand in front of Oliver. "You, on the other hand, are exactly what I expected. It's nice to finally meet you in person after all these years."

He punched Oliver in the stomach before he could respond. Morgan yelled out a strangled, "No!" as he doubled over. She pulled toward him, trying to wrench her hands free, but the guard behind her yanked her back.

Faraj patted Oliver on the side of the face when he straightened. "You cost me a lot of money and a lot of good men. I should shoot you now. But I'm feeling rather generous these days. You see, I've had some good fortune."

"Lucky you," Oliver grunted, still trying to regain his breath.

"Luck had nothing to do with it, I can assure you." Faraj's attention lifted past Oliver. "Arthur, good timing. Come in." He turned and walked behind the desk.

"There's something I wanted to show you, Oliver, but I wanted to wait for our friend to arrive."

He opened a drawer and carefully lifted out a plain wooden box, setting it on the desk. After lifting the lid, he turned it to display the contents for the rest of the room.

"I see," Oliver said, shaking his head at the rainbow of jewels in the box. "You were after my gems."

"It's only fair. And I appreciate your contribution to our cause," Faraj said, picking up a blue rock and examining it before putting it back and closing the lid just as Arthur joined him at the desk.

"So we didn't lose the cargo after all," Oliver said, "I take it you were the reason the boat sank then?"

"An old wreck like that? It wasn't hard to pop a plank."

"Surely it takes more than that to sink a boat."

"Well, sure. I had to destroy the bilge pump."

"And the dead man?"

"He discovered the pump had been tampered with, and I couldn't let him take that back to the captain 'cause then it would have gotten back to you, and you would have known something was up. Besides, it was cute watching you take the blame."

Oliver's jaw tightened. "And what about the other person?"

"What other person? I only killed one man on that ship. Give me some credit."

"No, at Wright and Lavigne. I know there was at least one other person involved in my attempted assassination."

"Oh, *that* other person. Eve. That poor sad woman. Did you know her husband is a total bore? She was begging for an affair. It only took about a week before she was madly in love with me and would do whatever I asked."

Morgan lunged for him. "You son of a — " She was jerked backward so hard her words strangled in her throat.

"Touchy." He took a step closer to her and tipped his head. "But isn't that what women want?" Arthur needled like a schoolboy.

Oliver grunted. "I wouldn't be too cocky, Arthur. She's the one who disabled all your plans."

Faraj cleared his throat. "Ah yes, very nice segue. Thank you, Oliver. I warned Arthur something like this would happen." He tapped a finger on top of the desk in thought. "If he hadn't insisted on planning your murder right under your nose, we wouldn't be standing here right now." His gaze traveled to Oliver as he spoke to the other man. "Arthur, was it as amusing as you'd hoped?"

"Yes it was," Arthur said.

"How about the time you sent me an email that led them right to me? Was that also amusing?"

Arthur's jaw shifted to the side. "I sorted it out — "

"No!" Faraj slammed his hand on the desk. "*I* sorted it out."

Arthur's response was quiet. "I did bring you Morgan."

"Nearly messed that one up, too, though, didn't you?" Oliver said.

Arthur flinched.

"Would you care to elaborate?" Faraj asked. His voice was eerily calm.

Morgan took a shot at Arthur when he didn't respond. "I found the email he sent yesterday."

"Hey, I did everything just like you asked me to," Arthur said quickly to Faraj. He had been arrogant when he entered the room, but it was clear he was afraid. "I got them here, didn't I?"

"I have to admit" — Faraj put a hand on Arthur's shoulder but was addressing the room — "Arthur is a clever schemer. He's the sort of man who would stab anyone in the back if it proved to be for his benefit. I've admired that about him and used it to my advantage, but … " He stepped back and nodded at one of the guards, who pulled out a pistol and shot Arthur in the head.

Morgan screamed and ducked her face away.

Oliver focused on the corpse and shook his head before closing his eyes. "What a waste," he said under his breath.

"I thought you'd enjoy that more," Faraj said as two of the guards dragged the dead man out.

"That was for my enjoyment?"

"You Americans are so sentimental. He had become a liability, obviously." Faraj tugged on his suit coat, straightening it. "I've got some things I need to see to, but I'm not done with either of you yet. We'll continue this later."

He waved a hand at the remaining guards. "Take them upstairs."

Chapter 25

MORGAN AND OLIVER were untied and pushed into a room with a rusty bed frame on one side and a wooden table on the other. Paint was peeling off every wall. The guard slammed the solid metal door shut with a loud clang that reverberated through the room.

Morgan leaned against the back wall and sank to the floor, wrapping her arms around her knees.

Oliver dragged the bed under a small window, high on the wall. He put a foot on the rusty frame to test it, then climbed up, reaching for the bars in the window. He gave them a shake, but they didn't budge. Then he gripped them hard and pulled himself up so he could see out, but the only view was the side of another building.

Morgan watched as he walked calmly to the door and tried the handle. He didn't turn back around straight away.

"No magically unlatched doors this time?" Morgan

said, her fingers reaching for the pendant Peter's wife had given her.

"It wasn't magic last time, you know," he said, turning.

She rested her chin on her fist. "I can't believe this is happening."

Oliver joined her on the floor. "I'm sorry."

"It's not your fault, by the way." She looked him in the eye.

"I didn't say it was."

"But you're thinking it. You want to take responsibility, don't you?"

He bit the inside of his cheek. "I shouldn't have let you come."

"It wouldn't have mattered. I would have come anyway. I'm a grown woman and it was my choice." She smiled, but it didn't reach her eyes, then she looked over at the locked door and let out a slow breath. "When they found me guilty, and I went to prison, I thought that was the worst thing that could ever happen to me." Her voice broke, and she looked away.

Oliver could see her body shake as she began to cry. He put his arm around her. No point avoiding it now.

She let him pull her in, and she wept into his shoulder.

"It'll be okay," he said into her hair.

She lifted her head and pushed a hand across her face to clear her eyes. "Is that what you really believe?"

His brows pushed together. "No."

"We're going to die, aren't we?"

"Probably."

"Unless your God does another miracle? For you anyway."

A spark of hope warmed his chest. "You don't think he'd do it for you?"

"Why would he? I'm not one of his followers."

"That's not a prerequisite. He's been chasing after you your whole life."

She managed a laugh through her tears. "Could be, but it doesn't matter now, does it?"

"Why not?"

"I'm under duress. If I told God I wanted him, it would be because I'm afraid and that doesn't count."

"It all counts."

She shook her head and leaned into him. He held her tighter, unsure how his feelings for her could be so strong in this moment.

"When do you think they'll kill us?" she asked.

The question was half-hearted and probably rhetorical, but he wished she hadn't asked it. He was certain he would die, but her fate could be much worse. He considered telling her so she would be prepared, but he couldn't bear to even form the words with his mouth. *God, please. Give her a miracle.*

He was relieved when he felt her sagging into him, her breathing slowing. He reveled in the small moment of peace while he watched the sun's light dim through the high window. Perhaps this was a small gift before the end.

A bang on the door startled them both awake. A sliver of morning sky shone through the window as a guard entered the room while two others waited in the hall.

Oliver and Morgan struggled to their feet. "You," the guard said, pointing to Morgan. "Come with me."

Oliver lunged in front of her. "No. I'll go."

"Oliver, no," Morgan said, but stayed behind him.

The guard took an aggressive step forward. "I wasn't told to bring you. I was told to bring her."

Oliver reached behind and touched her arm. "You'll have to go through me to get to her."

"Oliver," Morgan said, barely above a whisper. "Don't."

"Have it your way." The guard motioned to the others who entered the room and attacked.

Morgan screamed but was thrown back against the wall. Her head contacted it hard enough that she lost focus and slid to the ground, dizzy.

Oliver got in a few punches, injuring one of the men so that he had to pull back, but in the small space, he didn't have a chance. It wasn't long before they had him on the ground and were hammering him with blows. Morgan kept screaming at them to stop but could do nothing else but watch the nightmare.

They moved to kicking him with their heavy boots as he squirmed in a pointless attempt to protect himself.

When he stopped moving, the lead guard put a hand up for them to stop, but the man Oliver had injured gave one last kick to his ribs before they grabbed his arms and dragged him out of the room, leaving a small trail of blood. "We'll come back for you later."

Morgan stayed pressed against the wall with her mouth gapping in a silent scream. Tears continued to make a path down her face, dripping to the floor. She couldn't make herself move until the door was shut. Then she ran at it, stumbling as she went, and pummeled it with her fists, screaming again until her voice was hoarse and her hands bruised.

When she finally stopped, she pressed her forehead against the cool metal and slapped a flat hand against it with the small amount of fight she had left.

"No … Please … No. God, do something … Please. He's given everything to you. Don't make him go through this again. Please don't let them hurt him anymore. Please."

She sagged to the floor. "Please, Jesus. Please. Please, God." She rocked as she pleaded, "Don't let this happen. If you really helped Oliver before, then you can help him again."

The silence was deafening.

"Are you even listening?" she howled at the ceiling. "Why would you save him as a child just to make him go through it all over again? What is wrong with you?"

She waited.

Nothing.

"Do you even listen to people who don't believe in you?"

Oliver said God had been chasing after her her whole life. If that were true, then he must be listening.

She took a calming breath. It quivered as she blew it out. Maybe he didn't like to be yelled at. "Please, God. If you're real, I need you right now. I can't do this alone." She tried to swallow back her fear, but it wouldn't budge. "I just ... I can't ask for your help without the fear. I'm only talking to you now because I'm terrified. I'm sorry if it doesn't count, but I can't help it."

A yell echoed through the building.

"No!" She clapped her hands over her ears. "Please make it stop. I don't know what to do."

She was sobbing now, struggling to form her words. She fought through the fog of emotion, trying to remember what Miss Richardson had said, but her mind wasn't cooperating. She could only remember snippets.

"Please Jesus, please ... Come into my heart." She grunted in frustration when she couldn't remember anymore. "It's something to do with your blood." Her mind cleared for a moment. "You died. That's right. You died because I should have died, or I am dead. I can't remember ... No, I'm alive right now, but I don't want to die without you ... I deserve to die, but I don't have to. Not forever. I need you. I'm sorry and I need you." Even as the words left her mouth, they sounded stupid and childish, and she had no idea if they were even the right words, but her heart seemed to know what she meant. It swelled and tightened all at the same time, and even though the fear hadn't left, she didn't feel so alone anymore. She pushed her knuckles across her face to wipe some tears away and crawled over to the wall, settling her back against it.

After several deep breaths her emotions settled and she realized she had been expecting more. A miracle of some sort. Perhaps God hadn't accepted her.

She rested her head on her knees and must have fallen asleep because it seemed no time had passed when she heard the guards returning. Her head shot up before she stood, ready to hold her ground, surprised at her courage.

The door opened, and they threw Oliver onto the floor, then slammed the door shut.

His face was swollen and bloody. It looked like his arm was out at an odd angle, and he didn't move.

Morgan dove for him, touching him gently on his good arm.

"Oli? Are you okay?" She leaned over him, her cheek close to his mouth to check his breathing.

At first, there was nothing, but then she felt a breath and gasped in relief.

She sat back on the floor to assess his condition, not that she knew any way to help him. But God would know. If he cared.

She reached out and touched his face. "God?" she whispered. "Is there anything you can do here?" She pulled her hand back and watched Oliver, but there was no change. Of course there wasn't. What was she expecting?

The door clanged open again and she resisted the urge to grab hold of Oliver for protection.

"Your turn," said the guard.

She slid backward. "No. Leave me alone."

He marched over, kicking Oliver's leg out of the way as he went, and latched on to her arm, hauling her to her feet.

The terror returned and ripped through her body. "No." She thrashed her arms and legs. "I won't go."

As they dragged her through the door, in desperation she locked her fingers around the door frame until another guard came around and punched her in the stomach, knocking the wind out of her. It was a few seconds before she could suck in another breath and that was enough to eject the fight out of her.

She half-heartedly reached for the handle of a passing door but let it go as soon as she got hold of it. She didn't want to be punched in the stomach again.

They carried her back into Faraj's room, which was empty when they entered.

"Sit in the chair," the guard commanded, dropping her into it.

She obeyed, but fear coursed through her body in sickening waves, her mind contriving horror images of what was coming next. All the hope left her as she realized that God had rejected her.

When Faraj entered the room carrying a platter of food and set it on the table in front of her, the smell cleared her mind.

He watched her silently before letting out a long, sad sigh. "You're trembling."

He reached for her, but she jerked back against her chair.

"They've been too rough. I'm sorry for what happened to Oliver. If there had been any other way, I would have taken it, but my men must know I am strong. But please understand, it is not what I want. I am a man of peace. Truly."

"You're a liar."

He sat across from her and leaned his elbows on his knees, lacing his fingers. "We live in a world that only understands violence and so I must play by its rules. But the outcome I strive for will always be peace." He pushed the tray closer to her. "Please, eat. You must be starving."

She didn't expect to have an appetite amid everything that had happened, but the smells coming from the table made her mouth water.

Her eyes flitted between Faraj and the tray and she rubbed her fingers together then leaned forward. But as her hand reached out, a warning spread warm through her chest, and her arm recoiled.

Faraj frowned. "Not to your liking? I'm sure I can find some western food that may be more to your taste, but I would recommend giving this a try first. I can assure you, this is much better. Then perhaps we can talk about finding you more suitable accommodations."

Morgan's eyes widened as the warmth gave way to a feeling like cool water was being poured over her head. A tingling sense of clarity moved down her body and took her fear with it.

She held her breath for a moment when she grasped what Faraj was doing. She looked at him, her brows drawing closer. Then she looked at the food. The manipulation. He wasn't the first one to use the appearance of kindness to control her.

"I'm not hungry."

Faraj sighed and folded his hands in his lap. "You have no idea what I've done for you already." His voice was sharper now. It carried a foul edge. "You're very beautiful, and I have ordered my men not to molest you. But I can't protect you if you don't cooperate. It has been too long since they have seen an attractive woman."

Fear pricked at her spine but wasn't consuming her again.

"Miss Caine, I want to keep you safe, but you must work with me."

She forced herself to look Faraj in the eye. "Do what you must, but I will always be your enemy."

His face reddened and he stood. After tugging at his sleeves, he approached her, nostrils flaring, and slapped her hard across the face.

Pain cut through her mouth, and her vision blurred. She tucked her tongue into the side of her cheek and tasted blood.

She forced a smile from somewhere deep inside she didn't know existed until that moment. "I know people like you. You're nothing more than a bully, too self-absorbed to realize what a sorry little man you are."

His hands fisted at his side and she flinched at the expected attack, but none came.

"I could tell you had spirit, but after everything that's happened, I wasn't expecting you to be so stubborn. Or stupid. I can only assume it is because you think you have the same rights in this country as you do in your own, or perhaps you're waiting to wake up from a dream. That's fine. We have ways of helping you to understand the reality that you now find yourself in."

He went to the desk and pulled a knife out of the drawer. It had an ornate handle and a curved blade.

"What's that phrase they use in America? You're not in Kansas anymore?"

He lifted the knife and twisted it so it caught the light. Then the phone rang and his lips puckered. He tipped the knife at her, then stuck it into the desk as he answered the call.

He listened for a minute, taking in a sharp breath. "I'll be right there." He hung up the phone.

"Taair," he yelled at the door.

The guard entered. "Take her back up. I'll have to finish this later."

Taair wrapped a handful of her hair around his fist to keep her from causing him any trouble and dragged her from the room.

She had no intention of fighting him. She was too distracted by what had just happened. The warmth and cold. The phone call. Her courage and her relief.

Had God protected her? And if he did, could he save them? Was he saving them? Or was that too much to ask?

There was a moment with Faraj when she was sure she could infuriate him enough to expect a quick end to her suffering, but God had changed things. Or had he?

She was ready to die. In those few moments of clarity with Faraj, she knew the end was coming, but she had a strange peace about it. Perhaps it wouldn't last, but it didn't matter. It wouldn't be long until the end, so she held on to the belief that her new faith was a life raft that would bring her into eternity.

Chapter 26

THE GUARD SHOVED Morgan into the room and heaved the door shut. It clanged and bounced on the frame, remaining open.

Morgan ignored it. Turning from the door, she dropped down to check on Oliver.

He was breathing, but still unconscious. Her hands moved to his face, gliding across the bruising. They lingered for a moment before she reached for his good shoulder and squeezed it, hoping for a response, but there was none. Thoughts of brain damage and coma ricocheted through her mind, and she tipped her head up toward the ceiling. She looked around the room as she attempted to settle on something that wouldn't elicit the fear she was fighting. It shouldn't matter that he was unconscious. They would both die, but there was a part of her that couldn't let him go.

Her eyes strayed across the room and landed on the open door. She stared at it, waiting for it to clang shut, but everything remained quiet.

She checked Oliver again, then stood slowly and crept toward the opening, only going far enough so she could reach out and touch the middle of the door with her fingertips.

After letting out a controlled breath, she slid sideways, a fraction closer, and pushed the door open another inch before yanking her arm back to her side.

When there was still no response, she took another sidestep and pressed the door open far enough that she could get a view out into the empty hall.

Go.

The sound of the voice in her head startled her. It was only a thought, but it was loud, insistent and, she was convinced, was her own.

Her knuckles turned white as she fisted them to her side. After taking a big breath that she now held, she slid her toe across the threshold, then leaned out to peer down the other end of the hall. It was deserted but didn't feel like freedom to her. It felt like a trap. The unknown was more terrifying than her reality, and fear twitched the muscles up her back and sucked the air from her lungs. She scooted backward into the room until she bumped the back wall.

I can't do it. I can't go out there. Her whole body buzzed, and she crouched to the ground, shaking. Her fingers wrapped around the pendant, and she rubbed her thumb across the back of it.

A breeze blew through the room and cooled her hot face. She recoiled from it.

No. Don't make me do this. I can't do it. At least in the cell, she knew what to expect.

She squeezed the pendant and her thumb pressed into the latch, springing it open. Her eyes drifted down to the unfolding panels.

There was only one part with the words exposed: *"Please, Lord, save me!"*

She looked up at the open door, then back at the verse, pulling it open so she could read it aloud. "Death wrapped its ropes around me; the terrors of the grave overtook me ... Then I called on the name of the Lord: 'Please, Lord, save me!'"

She squeezed her eyes closed until she heard Oliver mumble something, then she groped across the floor to him. "Oli? Are you okay? Did you say something?"

His eyes remained closed, but he spoke again, his voice raspy. "Then I called on the name of the Lord."

"Yeah, that's right. 'Please, Lord, save me.'"

"How kind the Lord is. How good he is ... "

She waited for more, but he was silent. She read the verse over again, then focused on her hands, which were no longer trembling. The fear was still there, but she felt as if she could function again. She stood while she folded up the pendant, staying close to Oliver.

I don't know what's waiting outside that door, but I won't leave him. She wasn't sure if that was an excuse or a request. Oliver groaned.

Morgan took a deep breath. *Okay, God, here's the deal ... if I'm even allowed to make deals.* She winced but continued with her negotiations. *If I can get Oli on his feet and take him with me, I'll go. Otherwise, I'm staying here.*

She squatted down and slipped her arm under his good one and lifted, attempting to hoist it over her shoulders, but he was so much bigger than her and all dead weight.

She whimpered and dropped his arm gently back to the floor. "Come on, Oli, we need to go." She settled it in her mind that she wouldn't leave him behind. "Please. I need you to help me here. I can't leave you. I won't leave you."

God, you need to make me stronger, or you're going to have to take some of the weight. That's the only two options as far as I can see.

She tugged again, and Oliver groaned, then shifted and pushed himself onto his knees. Morgan laughed in surprised relief and positioned herself next to him to take some of his weight as he attempted to stand.

He rose from the ground, then fell to the side, crushing her against the wall. Morgan grunted. *Come on.* She looked into his face. His eyes were closed.

She pushed back and got him upright, then stumbled toward the door, using her foot to shove it fully open. She had intended to pause and check if it was safe to enter the hall, but the momentum carried them across he threshold and they crashed into the opposite wall.

Morgan grimaced at the pain lancing through her shoulder but didn't waste time getting them moving again. The hall was still clear, but each second held the tension that in the next moment, everything would change for the worse.

Oliver managed a limp, but his weight pressed heavily onto Morgan. Each time she checked his face, he still appeared to be unconscious.

Voices came from the adjoining hall up ahead and

Morgan tightened her arms around Oliver, pulling him to a stop. His weight fell against her again and pinned her to the wall as they waited to be discovered.

There was nowhere to hide, and it was impossible to move anywhere fast. She remained still and waited for fate to take its course.

Please, can we have a quick death? I don't want to know about it.

The voices grew louder. They weren't speaking English, but Morgan could translate the agitation and anger in the unknown words.

Two men hurried across the corridor. They didn't look anywhere but at each other as they talked. Then they were gone.

Morgan tipped her head to see the last of their retreat and her mouth turned up in a gapping smile of relief.

It took her a moment to settle her nerves. Once she was prepared to move again, she pushed on Oliver, but he wouldn't shift. She shoved again, but his body was like a wall, pinning her down. She gritted her teeth and pressed as hard as she could, finally getting him back upright.

When they reached the next hall, she couldn't stop to check if it was clear. Her body was now shaking from the effort, her strength diminishing quickly, so she continued on, half dragging Oliver around the corner.

"Oh no." She staggered to a stop, angling Oliver so he fell against the wall instead of immobilizing her again. *I forgot about the stairs.* Tears pressed hot at the back of her eyes. There was no way she could get him down safely. They were stuck.

Her body leaned against his to keep him from sliding down the wall while hopelessness bloomed in the pit of her stomach.

She considered their options. They could stay here and wait to be discovered or go back to the room.

Her eyes flicked up to the ceiling in a quick plea for help.

Did you bring us all the way out here, just to die in the stairwell? At least in the room, there had been the illusion of security.

But what difference did it make? This was as good a place to die as any. She yanked Oliver back onto her shoulder, and the two scooted sideways so she could grab the railing for support and lower him to the floor. But as she nudged him to the side, his foot lurched out, and he toppled forward, nearly taking Morgan with him.

She yelped, grabbing hold of the railing with one hand and wrapping her fingers around his shirt with the other.

The shirt tore out of her fist as she tried to haul him toward her, but it was enough to change his direction so he slid down the stairs feetfirst instead of headfirst. His injured arm was stretched out above him and cushioned his head as he fell. She hurried after him.

There was no way to tell if he'd suffered further injuries. She looked back up the stairs, then up at the ceiling. *Seriously?*

He moaned and rolled sideways. "Okay. Come on,

Oli. I need you to get up for me one more time. You did it before ... " Her words were smothered as she attempted to lift him again. Her arms felt like jelly and even though she got him on his feet again, her legs were close to collapsing. Each step had become an individual effort. The physical strain, along with the mental exhaustion, made movement close to impossible.

There was no reason for them to continue, but she kept moving. Her eyes remained focused on the floor in front of them. *Just ... one ... more.*

She slid her leg forward, but then stumbled against the wall, out of breath. It was everything she could do to keep them upright. But when she lifted her eyes, ready to give up, she found that the front entrance was just ahead.

Close to a dozen guards had been posted out front, from what she could remember. This was the end of the line for them.

She recalled Oliver's words about when he escaped as a child. He wanted to die free, not in a cage. God was answering that prayer now.

"I'm sorry, Oli. I can't save you in this life, but at least I can make sure, after all these years, you get to die free."

Tears filled her eyes as she thought about all the things she would never get the chance to do. When she left prison, she had felt as though there was nothing left for her in this life. Why did it take her facing death to figure out how much more life she had to live? At least she had eternity now.

She gripped Oliver's sides and pulled him away from

the wall so she could lead him to the front door. A new strength rose within her. She was ready to expend every ounce of the strength she had left, just to make sure they could see the sky before the end.

"You ready?" she asked Oliver, who didn't respond.

When they reached the door, she used her elbow to push the bar to open the door, and they stumbled out into the sunshine. Her eyes closed against the glare and she steadied the two of them as they walked out, waiting for the gunfire to erupt or at least the shouting. She was ready. She wasn't going to back down.

But there was only the muffled sound of nearby traffic. She blinked her eyes and squinted with one eye open a crack.

The courtyard was empty, and the front gate was ajar.

She looked throughout the courtyard, but there was no one. She refused to allow her thoughts to deliver hope. She couldn't think about living yet. Not yet. But she began moving again, somehow pulling Oliver along, their feet scraping in the dust as they headed for the open gate. Morgan's eyes continued to dart around the space. Waiting. Knowing that at any moment the enemy could appear.

When they passed through the gate, hope pressed into her mind again, but her energy was spent. They stopped at the road and both collapsed on the ground. She twisted around to look back through the gate.

Before walking out of the building, she had no strength left and yet somehow they'd made it all the way to the street.

It wasn't a busy road and when a car finally came past, Morgan could barely lift her arm to get the attention of the driver. But it didn't matter. The man kept his eyes averted and was out of sight without a second look.

Morgan wasn't deterred. Hope had taken root. They shouldn't have made it this far, and God wouldn't have brought them out here for nothing.

But as the hours passed, and after another dozen cars refused to stop, the fear was returning again.

With the sun now high and hot, she gave up trying to get help and instead dropped beside Oliver, hovering over his head to keep the sun off him.

She didn't know how much time had passed when she heard an engine slow. She looked up as a blue car came to a stop several feet away. The driver, a small man with glasses, got out, jogging around to them.

"Are you okay? Do you need help?"

Morgan opened her mouth, but tears choked off her words.

"Are you Americans?"

Morgan nodded, and he ran to open the back door of his car. He didn't look strong, but he took most of Oliver's weight as they dragged him into the car and laid him across the back seat.

Morgan got in beside the driver. Her voice barely audible, she said, "Thank you."

"Don't thank me yet. It looks like your friend is in bad shape. I think it's best if I take you to the American Embassy."

"Wait. Do you know this area well?"

"Yes."

She repeated the address for the compound, and he confirmed he could take them there.

"My name's Ibrahim," the man said.

"Oh … um, I'm Morgan."

"You okay? I guess that's a stupid question."

"No. Well, physically I'm fine. I mean, I don't know. Oliver's the one who's injured."

"Looks like you got yourself into some serious trouble."

"Yeah." She didn't want to get into the specifics. "How did you know we were Americans?"

"You look American."

"I didn't know we had a look."

"Oh yes." He looked at her and nodded his head. "American's definitely have a look. I went to school there, you know."

"You did?"

"Yes."

"But you came back here?"

"This is where my family is."

"What did you study in America?"

"Education. I'm a teacher here now."

"That's really nice." For some reason, knowing that made her feel better.

Scattered conversation filled the rest of the drive. But in the silent moments, her thoughts returned to Oliver. She reached her hand back and found his, gripping it tightly.

Chapter 27

WHEN THEY TURNED onto the familiar street of the compound, Morgan's heart was pounding out of her chest.

"This the place?" Ibrahim asked as he pulled up outside the gate.

"Yes! Thank you so much. I don't know why you've been so kind to us. But I'm so thankful for you."

"Do unto others," he said and winked.

She gave him a second look as she opened her door. "Will you wait here for a second?" She jumped out of the car and attempted to jog to the guard who was manning the gate, but her legs were stiff and sore and would only allow her a limp.

The guard lifted his radio to his face while he watched her approach. He didn't have a gun pointed at her, but he had it ready.

"I'm Morgan Caine," she called out as she drew near. He didn't look familiar to her.

"Can I see some ID?" he said with a British accent.

Her head dipped. "It's actually inside that building." The look on his face made it clear he didn't believe her. "Look, I've got Oliver Wright in the car. He's injured and in need of medical care. It's an emergency. Please."

"I'm sorry, ma'am, but I'll need to see some ID. You can't enter this premises without authorization."

"Please. I don't know how bad he is. You can come have a look for yourself. It's Oliver Wright. You know him, right?"

"I'm sorry, ma'am, I do not."

"Then can you get on your radio and ask Peter Black to come out. He'll be able to explain."

The guard observed her for a minute, then looked at the car. Ibrahim was standing behind the door, drumming his fingers on the top of the frame.

"Peter Black?" he asked, finally.

"Yes."

He spoke into the radio but must have had an earpiece because she couldn't hear the response. He turned his attention back to Morgan. "I'm sorry, but Black is not available at present."

Morgan ran a hand over her head and grabbed a fist full of it in frustration. "What about Michaels or Rodriguez? Please, this is an emergency."

"I'm sorry, ma'a — "

"Stop ma'aming me. An alarm went off — what was it? " She rubbed at her eyes, trying to remember the passing of days. "A day or two ago? Oliver and I were abducted by Arthur — " She grunted in frustration. "I can't remember his last name, but it doesn't matter. You need to do something or else Oliver is going to die, and I didn't go through all the trouble of getting us free so he could die."

She was close to hysterics, and the guard lifted his gun a degree. She took a step back and shut her mouth. He lifted the radio again and said something imperceptible, then put both hands on his rifle. "Ma'am, I'm going to have to ask you to leave. The American Embassy is close by. You can get help for your friend there."

A side door to the compound opened, and three people emerged. One of them was Rodriguez. They were all carrying weapons.

"Thank you, God," Morgan breathed out. Then she called out, "Rodriguez." She waved and the guard in front of her trained his gun on her. Morgan put her hands up and took another step back as the three newcomers jogged toward them.

"Caine? Is that you?" Rodriguez said when she got close. "I can't believe it. Is Black with you?"

"No. We managed to escape and Ibrahim brought us here — Why, where's Peter?"

"Out looking for you and Oliver."

"Well, he didn't find us, but I've got Oliver in the car and he's not good. He needs a doctor."

Rodriguez turned her attention to the guard. "Open the gate, Fowler. They're cleared."

"Yes, ma'am," he said and did as he was commanded.

Morgan motioned for Ibrahim to enter, and she followed the others to the building while Rodriguez radioed for a medical team to meet them outside.

After loading Oliver on a stretcher, they took him away.

Morgan attempted to follow, but Rodriguez held her back. "They'll look after him. Why don't you come inside with me? You hungry?"

Morgan nearly fainted at the mention of food.

Rodriguez directed her to the mess hall that was empty except for two people sitting at a table in the corner.

"I'm going to get someone to have a quick look at you, okay? We'll need to have a debrief with you, but that can wait. You want me to get you something?"

Morgan shook her head but fell into a nearby chair and didn't think she'd be able to stand again. Rodriguez patted her shoulder and left to find her some food.

Morgan rested her head in her hands, allowing herself to relax for the first time.

"You okay if I leave you here for a little bit?" Rodriguez asked after depositing a meal in front of Morgan.

"Yeah, I'm good. But can you make sure someone comes to tell me how Oliver is doing?"

"Of course."

Morgan ate a few bites, but found it wasn't settling in her stomach, so she opted to sip on a cup of tea instead. Exhaustion soon swept over her and she laid her head down on the table. She needed to stay awake so she didn't miss an update on Oliver when the time came, but she couldn't resist closing her eyes.

"Morgan."

It took Morgan a minute to pull back from sleep and focus on her body being shaken.

"Morgan, wake up."

She pried her eyes open, and when she finally came fully awake, she found Peter sitting beside her. She fell into him sideways, wrapping her arms around his neck and weeping.

He patted her back for a minute, then pulled her away. "Everything's going to be okay."

"Have you seen Oliver?"

"Yeah, I spoke to him before — "

"You did?" She made a move to stand, but Peter stopped her.

"He's not here anymore. They've transported him."

"Why didn't anyone come and get me?"

"It was a last-minute thing. There was a plane leaving, and they wanted Oliver on it. There wasn't time. He's headed back to the States and I'm here to escort you home."

Morgan pushed her face into her hands as she attempted to keep herself composed.

Peter rubbed her back. "Hey, everything is okay now. You're safe. You're both safe."

"I know." She sniffled. "I just … " She used her shirt to wipe her face. "I expected us both to be dead by now. So Oliver is going to be okay?"

"It appears that way. He'll have a lot of healing to do and they'll have to monitor him because of the concussion, but yes, it's looking good. He asked after you. I was glad to tell him you were safe and well."

"It was God. He saved us."

"God?"

"You don't believe me?"

"I was praying nonstop. I'm just surprised to hear *you* say it, is all."

Morgan nodded. "He and I are closer these days."

A sly smile snuck across Peter's face. "Then that's the best thing to come out of this by far."

Morgan's cheeks reddened, and she pressed her hands on them. "But when I say God saved us, I mean, really. Like the miraculous kind. The kind where the door gets left open, and the people disappear, and we walk out. Sort of. I mean, I dragged Oliver out. He was unconscious but was walking. It was crazy."

"Wow."

"I kept waiting for the miracle to end. For us to be shot dead, but it didn't. We walked right out the front door. I just couldn't believe it."

"I'm glad to hear I got to play a small part in God's miracle."

"What do you mean?"

"After we knew you'd been taken, we made a concerted effort to find Faraj."

"How'd you know we were taken?"

"When we couldn't find you and Oliver, Michaels told us what you had said to him. Your concern about Arthur. So we looked at the CCTV footage and saw what happened. We found one of Faraj's other hiding places. Not the one you were in, obviously, but I wonder if he sent a bunch of his guys to defend over there. Not to diminish the miracle. It still doesn't explain how you got out without being seen. At the very least, the door to your cell shouldn't have been left open."

"No … " Morgan wrapped her fingers around the pendant, lifting it. "And you can tell Jemi she was spot-on."

Peter's eyes darted to the ball. "Do you mind if I have a look?"

Morgan opened it for him. "I read it on the plane on the way over here and thought she was nuts."

Peter's eyes narrowed when he finished reading. "Now I know what she meant."

"About what?"

"She wouldn't tell me what it said, just that she was stepping out on a limb with this one. Said she really hoped she had heard God correctly."

"Don't blame her, but I'm glad she followed through. This was exactly what I needed to give me courage."

"You can tell her yourself if you like."

"How?"

"She's coming to New York. I didn't like the idea of you going back to your apartment just yet. Not with Faraj still on the loose. But I didn't want you at Oliver's by yourself, either, so I asked Jemi to stay with you, just to give you time to recover. The impact of something like what you've experienced doesn't dissolve overnight."

Morgan's eyes filled with tears again, and she slapped them off her face. "I'm getting tired of crying every five seconds." She sighed. "That's very generous of her. I look forward to meeting her."

Peter stood and took Morgan's hand, lifting her up.

"You should get to bed. You need your rest and we won't be leaving till the morning."

"When we get back home, can we go straight in to see Oliver?"

Peter shook his head. "We'll arrive after visiting hours."

"What? That can't apply to this situation."

"But it does. Don't worry, we'll get you in to see Oliver as soon as we can."

"I won't rest well until I can see for myself that he's okay."

He put his hand on her arm. "I understand, and we will get you in to see him as soon as we can, but it will have to be within visiting hours."

"Fine, but I don't like it."

"And you don't have to."

Morgan was wrong about not being able to rest. As soon as her head hit the pillow she fell into a dreamless sleep. She carried the lethargy onto the plane and was surprised when she woke up to find they were an hour from landing.

By the time they got back to Oliver's apartment, her body felt like it was being pressed down to the point that she expected to fall through the floor at any moment, but the mixture of aromas that met them at the door aroused her senses and reminded her that she was about to meet Peter's wife.

Morgan opened the door to find an elegant woman with long, dark hair standing behind the counter in the kitchen, pushing something sizzling around in the frying pan.

When she saw them enter, a smile lit her face and creased the corners of her eyes. "Peter ... Morgan." She whipped off her apron and scooted around to embrace them both.

"Jemi, I'd like you to meet Morgan," Peter said, dropping the bags at the door as he wrapped an arm around his wife.

Jemi gave him a quick squeeze and pushed him away so she could give Morgan a proper hug before stepping back to look her over. Her eyes paused briefly on the necklace before lifting and settling on Morgan's face. "It's a pleasure to meet you finally." Her Middle Eastern accent was still strong.

"It's wonderful to meet you, too. Peter has told me so much about you." Her dark eyes flicked to her husband with a look that Morgan couldn't decipher. Then they moved to the couch, where Jemi insisted they both sit down. "Peter, go stir that for me, would you?"

"Sure thing."

"I don't know if you're hungry, Morgan, but I'm making some dinner for us."

"I'm starving, actually. Thank you."

Morgan spent the rest of the evening swapping between shock and laughter as Jemi and Peter told stories from their lives. Some they shared together, others from further in their past. She couldn't remember having a better time.

Her experience in Libya had been the worst she'd ever had, but it felt as though it opened a door into her future that had previously been closed off to her, and it filled her with a hope she had never known.

Before going to bed that night, she googled the story of Paul after the light had blinded him. The scripture itself didn't speak to her on a deep level, but there was something about reading the Bible that made her feel whole from the inside out. She went to bed that night with peace in her heart and an assurance of a goodness that surpassed circumstances.

Chapter 28

WHILE IT WAS STILL DARK, Morgan padded into the kitchen to make herself a coffee. The end of her sleep had been fitful as images of Oliver's broken body played with her dreams just before she woke up.

The door between the two apartments had been left open in case Morgan needed anything in the night and it wasn't long before Jemi joined her for a coffee.

"You sleep well?" Jemi asked while getting her own drink.

"Most of the night, yeah. But then I started having some bad dreams. I'm okay though."

"You're eager to see Oliver."

"Yeah. I just need to see for myself that he's okay."

Jemi nodded and sat beside Morgan at the counter. "I like Oliver, but he's stubborn. Sometimes he can be so busy being stoic, he forgets to live."

Morgan smiled. "But he's a good man."

"A very good man." Jemi looked at Morgan. Her

eyes were intense and gave the impression she was reading Morgan's deepest darkest secrets.

Morgan felt compelled to explain away her comment before Jemi got any ideas. "When we were locked up, the guards came to take me away, but he wouldn't let them. Well, he wouldn't let them while he was conscious. He's in hospital now for his efforts, but it meant a lot."

Peter entered the room and Morgan was relieved to be out of Jemi's gaze.

"Good morning ladies," he said before giving Jemi a peck on the cheek. "Morgan, you doing okay up here?" He poked a finger into his temple.

"So far."

"What time do we leave for the hospital?" Jemi asked. "Morgan needs reassurance."

Peter didn't notice the coy look his wife was giving Morgan, or the fact that Morgan's focus was squarely on the contents of her mug. "I'm eager to see how he's doing too," Peter said before tipping back the rest of his coffee. "We'll go as soon as they'll let us in."

After what felt like decades, they all finally made it to the hospital. When they reached Oliver's floor, Morgan had such an upheaval of emotions, she held back.

Jemi slipped her arm around Morgan's waist and pulled her aside before they entered the room.

"You okay?"

"Yeah, I don't know what's wrong with me."

"Nothing is wrong. You're dealing with trauma. It's

completely normal to feel overwhelmed at seeing Oliver. He'll likely feel the same."

"You think so?"

"Trust me, you have nothing to worry about. This is possibly the only time in your life you can excuse away any kind of crazy behavior. So take advantage of that if you need to."

Morgan took a deep breath. "Right, okay. Thank you, that helps."

"Good. Then let's go see how our friend is doing."

Peter was first to enter while Jemi held Morgan's hand, giving her little comforting squeezes.

Oliver was looking at his phone and only lifted his eyes to see who had entered, but when he saw who it was, his mouth lifted into a painful smile. His face was still bruised and swollen in places and his arm was in a sling, but he was alert and his eyes were clear.

"Hey, you're looking better," Peter said, pressing a hand onto his friend's shoulder before moving aside so Jemi could give him a kiss on the cheek.

Then it was Morgan's turn. She leaned in to give him a gentle hug, then laughed nervously. "Don't want to hurt you."

"After all we've been through, you could kick me and I don't think I'd mind. It's so good to see you, Morgan. Peter told me you were okay, but I think I needed to see for myself."

"Me too. I wasn't sure how bad you were."

"Amazingly well, considering. But my shoulder is pretty messed up."

"At least it helped cushion your fall," Morgan said before she realized what she was saying.

"I'm sorry?" Oliver said.

Peter leaned in. "What's this?"

Morgan tried to smile her comment away, but it turned into a lopsided wince. "You fell down the stairs. Because of the odd angle of your arm, it cushioned your head while you went down."

"I don't remember that."

"No. You weren't conscious. I wasn't even going to go down, but then you just suddenly pitched forward. You were lucky you didn't go down headfirst."

Jemi held back a laugh and turned her head away to hide her smile.

"When was this?"

"When we were escaping."

Oliver looked at Peter. "You didn't tell me this."

"Hey, I didn't know anything about it."

"I got us out, didn't I?" Morgan said, her forehead wrinkled in a frown.

Oliver reached for her hand. "You did amazing, and one day soon you'll have to tell me the whole story."

Peter clasped his hands behind his back. "Hey, Jemi, don't we have that thing to do?"

"The thing?"

"Yeah, remember?"

She paused like she was deciding something, and before responding, she looked at Morgan, who only looked confused.

"Yeah … the thing." Jemi smiled. "We'll be back soon."

"Thank you for saving me," Oliver said, bringing Morgan's attention back to him after the other two had left the room. "Peter didn't give me many details besides the fact that you got me out of there somehow."

Morgan sat in the chair by his bed. "Yeah, God left the door unlatched for you again."

Oliver blinked. "For us, you mean."

Morgan smiled into her lap. "Yes. For us."

"One question though."

"Yeah?"

"You said I was unconscious?"

"Yeah."

"Then how'd you get me out? I know you're tough, but I am a lot bigger than you."

"The door thing wasn't the only miracle. I couldn't lift you, so I gave God an ultimatum. He had to either make me stronger or take some of the weight."

"You gave God an ultimatum."

"Well, I'm new to this stuff. I didn't know if he'd help me out, but I was desperate. Thankfully, we got you to your feet."

Oliver pressed his lips together, processing her words before speaking. "You're new to what stuff?"

"Oh that. It turns out that Jesus does, in fact, fit in my heart."

"When did that happen?"

Morgan bit her lip. "When they were beating you up."

Oliver's eyes darkened, but then it passed. "Miss Richardson would be so proud."

Morgan looked down and put her hand over her heart. "Yes, she would."

"I'm sorry you had to go through all that, though. I knew I shouldn't have brought you."

"Oliver, you're driving me crazy. You have got to stop doing that. God brought something good out of the bad. Just like what happened to you as a kid. I might not have made my commitment to him if that hadn't happened. In fact, I know I wouldn't have."

Oliver sighed and changed the subject. "So, I walked out of there on my own two feet, huh?"

"Sort of. Like I said, it got tricky when we reached the stairs."

"And what, you just pushed me?"

She put her hands up in defense. "Hey, I already told you I wasn't going to go down. You're the one who made the first move." She laughed, glad she could laugh about something so horrible now. "I'm happy to see you looking better, though. There were a few times there when I thought I'd lost you."

Oliver reached up and ran a hand down her arm. "Morgan, I — " His words caught in his throat, and he retracted his fingers, resting his hand back on the bed, a distant look in his eye. "I'm glad things worked out as well as they did." He wouldn't meet her questioning look. "Thanks for visiting me, but I'm feeling pretty tired. I think I should rest."

"Oh." Morgan looked around the room, trying to figure out what had just happened. The sudden change in his mood bewildered her.

She stood. "Of course you would be. I'll go find

Peter and Jemi." She patted his arm and shuffled awkwardly around the chair before turning back to him to say something else, but all her words left her. She nodded and walked out the door without looking back again.

Oliver watched her go, then put a hand over his face. He had messed up. He should have protected himself from her better. Or perhaps he should have protected her from him. Now, after all they had been through, he was going to have to pay the price, knowing he had hurt them both.

Peter came back into the room a moment later and saw the cloud on Oliver's face. "Uh, hey. Just came across Morgan. Everything okay? She seemed a bit startled."

"Yeah it's fine. I'm just tired."

Peter studied his friend but decided to let it drop for the moment. "I just had a phone call from Libya and I've got some good news."

"Oh yeah?"

"When we left, I had them keep looking for Faraj. They found him, and they cornered him. He put up a fight, but in the end he was killed."

Oliver sniffed. "One out of the way to make room for the next."

"My, my, you're in a mood."

"Sorry. Lying in bed all day is getting to me."

"You sure that's what's eating at you?"

"That's good news," Oliver said, returning to the

original topic. "I'm glad to know we're safe now. Everything can go back to normal."

"Mmm. Normal. Well, I'm going to get going, but I'll check in on you later."

"Thanks for all your help."

"You know you can call on me anytime. For anything."

"You've been a good friend, Peter. Thank you."

Chapter 29

PETER AND JEMI helped Morgan shift back into her apartment now that the risk was gone. Camilla jumped on Morgan, nearly flattening her to the floor when she returned. She had been couch surfing, avoiding her mom at all costs, and was overjoyed to be back in her own space. Camilla had begun needling Morgan for details of her stay with Oliver, but quickly recognized things were not okay and was wise enough to let it drop.

Everything returned to normal over the next couple weeks, but for Morgan it was worse than when she had first left prison. Her new faith helped, and she found the Bible to be her new refuge, but she was more unsettled than she had been before and found it impossible to sit still.

Camilla tried to keep her from working at first, but Morgan needed the distraction and focused on doing her job the best she could. Even Sal had trouble finding a fault, and when Morgan began asking his opinion and complimenting him on his job, he softened to her and in a few short days became something of a friend.

Jemi informed her that Oliver was back at home, but he hadn't been in touch. She missed seeing him, but after the way he responded to her at the hospital, she was unsure how to proceed. And she was tired to death of going over their last encounter to try to figure out what she had done to cause him to pull away.

"I'm over him," she said to herself one afternoon as she rummaged through her allocated drawer in the bathroom.

"Hey, Cam, have you seen — " She looked at her hand and groaned. In her haste to pack, she had forgotten about the drawer in the bedside table at Oli's, where she had left her heart ring to keep it safe while she traveled to Libya.

She slammed the drawer shut in frustration. If it had been anything else, she would have left it.

"You okay in there?" Camilla called from the couch where she was painting her toenails. Morgan walked out into the fumes of the nail polish and went straight for the window, heaving it open and sticking her head out to take in a dramatic breath.

"You're in a mood," Camilla said, lifting her eyes off her work for a moment.

"Yeah," Morgan said, facing out to the street. "I'm going out."

"You're different, you know."

Camilla was looking at her toes when Morgan turned in surprise. "What do you mean?"

Camilla bounced her foot to dry the paint and looked at her friend. "You're lighter. And also more dramatic. Even after what happened in Libya. I still can't believe you went to Libya without telling me, by the way."

"Well, I don't feel light but I'll agree with the dramatic part."

"You seem less angsty than you were before too."

She hadn't yet told her friend about becoming a Christian. She was still trying to figure out what it meant for herself. "It's probably true. You don't go through a situation like that and come out the same." Besides that, the weight she now felt was more sad. Like she'd lost something special, and she knew she'd never get it back.

"Where are you going?" Camilla asked, starting on her other foot.

"I left something at Oli's."

"That wasn't on purpose, was it?"

Morgan shook her head vehemently. "No. Definitely not." Camilla had been passionately devastated when she discovered that Morgan and Oliver hadn't ended up together, and Morgan had appreciated her friends outrage, not feeling like she could express it openly herself. "I'd rather not go, but I left my ring."

"Is he going to be at home?"

"I don't know. I'm hope not. But there's no way for me to know."

"Good luck. And don't forget, I still think it's all because of his concussion. That's the only explanation."

"You're just saying that 'cause you still have a soft spot for him."

"So what if I do? I still think deep down he's a good guy, but that doesn't change my fury at his behavior."

Morgan rolled her eyes but hid her smile.

Oliver's building felt ominous as Morgan approached. *God, please don't let him be there.*

Inside the foyer, she found Roger on the phone.

"Can you hold for one minute?" he said into the phone when he spotted her. He dropped it down onto his chest. "Miss Caine, how lovely to see you again. Oliver said you had returned to your own apartment."

"Yes, I have. I've just left something behind that I need to get."

"Yeah, sure. Go ahead. Oliver's up there with Peter."

"Oh ... good. I, uh ... I don't have a key anymore though."

"Of course. Just a sec." Roger quickly finished his phone call, then walked with her to the elevator and tapped a card on the panel.

"Thanks, Roger."

She breathed out slowly as the elevator rose. God hadn't answered her prayer for Oliver to be away, but it was still something knowing Peter was there.

When the doors opened, she stepped onto the gray carpet and stopped for a moment. It still felt safe here. She shook her head. She didn't need that anymore.

The door to the apartment she had stayed in was locked. That had been her one chance to get in and out without being noticed. There was no avoiding it now, only getting it over and done with.

She knocked on Oliver's door and waited. Oliver pulled it open, a questioning look on his face that soon slipped into a smile. He still had some bruising, but his face was no longer swollen. "Morgan?"

"Sorry to disturb you."

"No, not at all. Please come in."

"Morgan," Peter said, embracing her. "I'm glad to see you. I'm heading back home today, so it's perfect timing."

"Great. Um, I … actually, I left something here. My ring." She pointed at her naked finger. "So I came over. Because I forgot it in the drawer. It's next door."

"Yes, of course," Oliver said. "Go ahead through."

"Thanks." She dipped her head and went to the internal door, scrunching up her face as she went through. She was acting like an idiot.

Peter cleared his throat and crossed his arms.

"What?" Oliver asked of Peter's cynical look.

"You going to do something about that?"

"Already have."

Peter looked at the door, then back at Oliver. "Really? 'Cause it doesn't look like it."

Oliver stuffed his hands in his pocket. "I don't need a lecture."

"Suit yourself."

Morgan returned. "Got it." She held up her hand

with the ring in place as though she needed to show the proof. "Well, I guess I'll say goodbye."

"Before you go." Oliver went to the piano and swiped up a business card that was lying on it. "You did so much for me these past couple of weeks. More than was required, actually. And I wanted to return the favor. At least in a small way."

"There's no need." She could do nothing to hide the flush that was rushing up her neck.

His voice softened. "But I want to." He walked over to her. "I have a friend who runs a small but very successful technology company in California. I told him about you, about how good you are, but also about your stint in prison and what a waste it would be to not see you used to your full potential. He is very interested in speaking with you. It would be an opportunity for you to start fresh where no one knows your past, except him, of course, and you can do what you love." He held out the card to her. "I've told him you'll call."

She took the card, but once it was between her fingers, it was a struggle to lower her arm again. "That's very thoughtful." She had to force out the words. "Thank you. I'll think about it." She tried to smile, but it was a pitiful attempt. "I guess I better get going."

She gave Peter another hug, but couldn't look him in the eye, afraid she'd start crying. Then she waved stiffly at Oliver and was gone.

Peter guffawed when the coast was clear. "What was that?"

"What? You don't think she deserves a second chance?"

Peter covered his face with his hands and grunted. "Oh, Oliver." His words were smothered by his palms that slid down far enough that he could peer at his friend through his fingers. "You are an idiot."

"Hey, Mark runs a fantastic company out there. She'd be a great fit."

"I'm sure he does, and yes, she would, but Mark's not the one who's in love with her."

"This has nothing to do with love."

"Oh, but I think it has everything to do with love."

"Peter."

"Tell me I'm wrong."

Oliver threw his good arm up in the air. "Okay, fine. You're right. It does have everything to do with love. I'm in love with Morgan, okay? But we can never be together, so we are both better off if we aren't in the same time zone."

"What do you mean, you can never be together? Why not — oh, wait." His face fell. "Is this because of that vow you made all those years ago?"

"Yes. I made a promise to God and I will not back out on it because I fell in love with some girl."

"I'm sorry, Oliver, but Morgan is not just *some* girl."

"It doesn't matter though, does it? I still made a promise."

Peter sighed and sat down on the edge of the couch, resting his elbows on his knees. "Look, Oliver, that promise you made after Theresa died was probably the right thing at the time. You needed to get your life sorted out, and swearing off women and alcohol was one of the best things that happened to you. But are you going to spend the rest of your life paying for sins that are already forgiven?"

"That's not what I'm doing, and it doesn't change the fact that Theresa died and it was my fault."

"Oliver, she killed herself."

"But she was depressed when she came to me, and I didn't want to deal with it, so I got her drunk to shut her up." He scoffed, "I shut her up all right."

Peter walked over to Oliver and put a hand on his shoulder. "And you've repented for that and been forgiven. You took the steps you needed to take in order to make sure nothing like that happened again. But you take on the weight of this stuff and forget that there is only one Intercessor qualified to carry that weight, and you're not him."

Oliver shrugged off Peter's hand. "I appreciate your concern, but you're lecturing again."

Peter put his hands up in surrender. "Okay. I've gotta go anyway, but I want you to promise me one thing before I go." Oliver clicked his tongue. "Promise me or I won't leave it alone."

"Fine, what is it?"

"I want you to have a conversation with God about this and make sure you two are still in agreement."

"We are."

"Just ask. For me. And make sure you listen. Think about what would have happened to Isaac if Abraham hadn't listened when God changed the plan once they were up that mountain."

Oliver squeezed his forehead. "Fine. I promise."

"I'll miss you, Oli. You make sure to come and visit Jemi and me some time."

"I will."

The two men embraced, and then Oliver was left on his own. He stood at the window with his arms wrapped around himself. "Okay, God, you heard him. You let me know what you think."

Peter's words drifted through his mind: *Are you going to spend the rest of your life paying for sins that are already forgiven?*

Oliver shook his head to remove the thoughts. "I don't need to hear you again, Peter."

He sat down at the piano and rested his fingers on the keys. He played the first couple of bars of "Moonlight Sonata," then stopped. If he didn't get busy, he'd spend the rest of the day brooding.

Chapter 30

OLIVER HAD KEPT himself busy at work over the next several days. They had to find a replacement for Arthur and deal with Eve. It wasn't a pleasant experience. He also went to war for a place in his business to do the work he was passionate about, finally giving Brian an ultimatum. If the man didn't like the direction Oliver was taking Wright and Lavigne, then he could resign with a healthy retirement package.

He avoided the restaurant where he met Morgan. Just in case. He couldn't risk seeing her again. It hurt too much. But every night when he returned home, he thought about her, wanting to talk with her about his day.

After returning home earlier than usual one afternoon, he flopped down on the couch in frustration. He expected things to get easier, for Morgan to take a back seat in his mind, but she wouldn't budge.

He leaned forward on his knees. "Okay, God. I've had about all I can take here. Was I wrong to keep my promise?" He leaned back. "No, of course I wasn't."

He held his breath and counted off the seconds before expelling it in one big blow.

"All right. I made a promise to Peter, too. So here we go. But keep Peter out of it. Just tell me plainly. Do I keep my word to you? Or do I let myself fall in love?" He sat quietly, waiting for any hint or whisper, but all that filled the room was silence. His mind was a void.

He stood and paced for several minutes, stopping at the window on each pass and looking into the sky that was changing color with the setting sun. But there was nothing. No sign or niggle.

He couldn't take the silence anymore, so he left the building and headed for the subway. He couldn't remember the last time he had used it, but his car would be too quiet and he couldn't stay where he was.

He bought a ticket for a suburb that sounded familiar, but he didn't know why and when the stop came, he raced aboveground, desperate for fresh air.

His steps were fast. It felt as though he were in a hurry to get somewhere, but he had nowhere to go.

As he passed a small park, he stopped and looked around. His eyes widened in recognition. He knew this place. Spinning around, he looked up the street.

He knew exactly where he was.

God, is this your doing or mine? Now he felt more conflicted than ever. *Please just tell me, so I can get on with life.*

He wanted to scream up at the sky, but then it came. A small thought dropped into his mind. *Stop resisting.*

Resisting what? Do I want Morgan so much that I don't want to hear that I have to give her up for good? Because I will. I already have.

Peter's words came back to him then. *Are you going to spend the rest of your life paying for sins that are already forgiven?*

Oliver rubbed his forehead. *How about something from your Word and not from Peter?*

I have come that you may have life …

Oliver took a moment and dared to imagine a life with Morgan. The anxiety eased immediately, and he felt the weight of fear lift. He remembered the psalm where David said that God had lifted him from the miry clay and that's what it felt like now. It was as though he had been drowning and now his head had come above water.

He looked up at the sky. "Seriously?" He laughed. "How can it be that simple?"

An old lady was walking her dog toward him. She stopped and turned around, hurrying off in the other direction. Oliver offered her a mental apology for looking crazy, then ran in the opposite direction until he reached Morgan's apartment building.

His finger paused, poised over the door buzzer, and he sent up one more offering. *You know I'll give her up for you. Don't let me make a mistake here.*

He felt no warning to stop. "Okay, here goes." He pushed the button.

A voice came through the static. "It's about time."

Then the door unlocked. Oliver nearly missed his opportunity to get through.

"Surely not," he said before opening the door. *How can she know I'm coming?* He raced up the stairs, full of hope.

When he reached Morgan's floor, he saw the door was open and Camilla was leaning against the door frame, picking at her nails. Her annoyance was obvious, but when she glanced up and saw Oliver, her mouth dropped open. "You're not pizza."

"No," he said, stopping several feet away. "I'm not."

"What are you doing here?" Her eyes narrowed.

"I'm here to see Morgan if she's home."

She gave him a good looking over, her eyebrow lifted in disapproval, then she moved into the apartment and waved him through.

The metal plate on the wall chirped an alert to the front door and Camila jumped for it. "You had better be my pizza. I'm starving."

"Uh, yes?" came the crackly voice on the other end.

She jammed her thumb on the button to unlock the door, then looked at Oliver. "Morgan," she yelled while still eyeballing him. "You have company."

Morgan came out of her room carrying a heavy suitcase with both hands. She stopped when she saw Oliver. "Hi." She set the suitcase down carefully as the pizza delivery guy arrived at the door.

"Finally." Camilla grabbed her food. "It's been over thirty minutes."

The guy looked at his watch. "Twenty-eight."

Morgan hurried over and dug a few dollars out of

her pocket to give him a tip. "You better go quick. She gets violent when she's hungry."

After stuffing the bills into his pocket, he didn't waste time retreating.

Camilla, holding on greedily to the pizza box, looked between the two of them. "I'll just, uh, take this into my room."

Morgan waited until Camilla was safely behind her bedroom door before speaking. "What are you doing here?"

"You're packing?"

"Yeah. I called your friend Mark. He made me an offer I couldn't refuse. And you were right. It will be good to start over somewhere new."

"Wait, what if you came to work for me instead?" He didn't know what else to say. He just knew he needed to change her mind.

"What?"

"You know its weaknesses. You could fix it. Stay here."

"But I've already told Mark I'm coming."

He took a tentative step toward her. "What if I made you a better offer?"

Morgan frowned and dropped her head. "I won't change my mind."

"Morgan — "

"No, Oliver. Stop. Please."

She pressed a hand against her cheek. If she made it plain for him, it would be easier for him to go, even if it was completely embarrassing and soul baring. But that didn't matter because she'd never see him again.

"I can't work for you. I don't want to work for you, because … "

She tipped her head up to the ceiling, trying to formulate the right words. She closed her eyes before looking at him again. "I know I'm not your type, and honestly, you're not mine."

Oliver's heart twisted in pain. He'd made a mistake. "I understand."

"No, you don't. Despite the fact that we come from two different worlds, somewhere along the line I fell in love with you." Oliver's jaw flexed. "And working for you would be a nightmare knowing you didn't feel the same. This job in California is the best thing for both of us. That way, neither one of us has to suffer more than necessary."

He started moving before she had finished speaking. It took him three steps to close the space between them before he put a hand behind her head and pulled her into a kiss.

Morgan's body filled with an explosive numbness that made it hard to breathe. She wanted to kiss him back, but she was completely immobilized.

He moved his hand to the side of her face when he pulled away.

Her eyes were wide. "What's happening?" she breathed.

"When I said you weren't my type, that was mostly to keep you at arm's length. I don't really want you to work for me. I don't know why I said that, but I do love you, Morgan Caine."

Morgan's body tingled as her senses returned. She grabbed the front of his shirt and shook her head. "Oli."

He slipped his hand back behind her neck and kissed her again. This time she wrapped her arms around him and kissed him back until there was a "Whoop!" from the other side of the room, and they ripped apart.

Camilla was leaning against her door frame, shoving a slice of pizza into her mouth. "I knew it," she said while chewing. "Didn't I? I told you Morgs. I told you I was a brilliant matchmaker." She held the pizza box out. "You two want any?"

Morgan grabbed a pillow and threw it at her friend, who watched it fall short. "Okay, but it's your loss." She disappeared again.

Oliver ran the back of his fingers over Morgan's wet cheek. "I made you cry."

"Good tears this time. But I don't understand. What was that job in California all about?"

Oliver groaned. "It's a long story that I'll tell you about another time."

"But you were trying to get rid of me."

"I was, because I didn't think we could be together and I couldn't stand the idea of having you close by if we couldn't be together."

"I'm glad you changed your mind."

"You can thank Peter. Hang on." He kept one arm around her while he pulled out his phone and sent a quick text:

You'll be pleased to know that I didn't kill Isaac.

Peter responded with a string of fireworks.

Oliver smiled and slipped his phone back into his pocket. "There is one thing that concerns me, though. I'm not sure whether we're going to get past it."

She pulled her head back in worry. "What?"

"Well." He grimaced. "Do you really think you can love a man who has a man bun?"

She punched him lightly in the stomach, then buried her face in his chest. He wrapped his arms around her. So much had changed in such a small amount of time.

"If there is one thing I've learned about you, Oliver, it's that there is nothing about you I can take for granted."

Epilogue

OLIVER OPENED the door to let Morgan enter the church ahead of him, remembering the first time they had come together. They had received a lot of looks and whispers, but Suzie had run straight up and introduced herself, warming to Morgan straight away.

"They've done an amazing job," Morgan said as she clasped her hands together and looked over the string of lights, warming the room with a soft glow.

"Oli!" Came a screech from the other side of the room and a white streak zoomed across the room and latched onto Oliver's leg. "You came."

"Wouldn't miss it for the world, Suz." He adjusted her halo that had slipped back on her head during the attempted tackle.

She let go of Oliver and moved on to give Morgan a quick squeeze. "So you're an angel, huh?" Morgan said, giving her an appreciative once-over.

"I even have a line." Suzie beamed.

"Oh, yeah? What's that?" Oliver asked.

"I can't tell yooouuu." She squirmed. "Gotta go." She sped off.

Morgan pulled her coat more tightly around her. "I'm gonna grab a blanket."

"I'll find a seat." On his way over to the chairs, he noticed Lauren waving him over.

"Oli, I'm so glad you made it. I think you've set a new record for your attendance these past couple months." Her eyes darted toward Morgan, who was lifting an afghan from the basket near the door. "She's a good influence on you."

"Well, she's a new Christian, so I wanted to make sure she had a solid start."

"Mm-hmm. But a new Christian with a lot behind her. She's really impressed me with her depth." Lauren and Morgan had become friends over the past few months after Oliver asked if Lauren could meet up to explain the basics of Christianity.

"How's that?"

"It's small things, like the questions she asks, like 'Why did Peter jump out of the boat to walk on water to confirm it was really Jesus?'"

"Isn't that what he asked Jesus?"

"Yeah, but she said he could have been a ghost that was pretending to be Jesus and then Peter would have been in trouble."

Oliver blinked. "That's very true. I never thought of that."

"Hey, Lauren." Morgan said when she joined them.

"You guys better grab a seat. It's filling fast. We'll catch up after."

. . .

Oliver stood with Morgan when the Christmas carols started the show, but he had to stop singing along as Morgan belted out a Christmas chorus she knew well. He couldn't get used to hearing her worship. When they first started coming along, she was timid in her singing, partly because she was new, but also because she didn't know the songs, but he knew she had a hidden talent for it.

She had the same folksy sound he had enjoyed from that first time her heard her sing, but hearing her worship was something else entirely.

He closed his eyes and just listened. It was his favorite time of the week. He knew he'd eventually get over this ridiculous infatuation, but it was really the first time he'd allowed himself to love someone, and he was embracing every moment of it that he could.

When they sat, Morgan laid the blanket across both their laps and leaned into him, watching the kids tell the story of Jesus's birth. It was the first Christmas she'd had from this perspective. She'd always found the Christmas story heartwarming, but never realized its significance until now and when the kids sang "Gloria in Excelsis Deo," she got tears in her eyes. These little ones who knew who Jesus was. She sent up a silent prayer that their faith would always be strong so they didn't find themselves far away from God like she did.

At the end of the show, everyone stood and cheered, the sound echoing off the walls in a somehow harmonious cacophony and the kid's faces beamed with pride.

Morgan and Oliver stayed long enough for hot cider and powdered donuts, Morgan's new favorite, and then Oliver took her hand and pulled her out into the day, heavy with clouds that were letting go of their contents.

Large snowflakes dampened the sound around them and Morgan lifted her head, attempting to catch one on her tongue. When she caught Oliver watching her with a strange smile, she gave him the evil eye. "What?"

Oliver shook his head. "You. You're so much ... different."

"Well, a lot has changed in my life over these past few months."

"I know, it's just strange to have fallen in love with you before and to now to be getting to know the real you. It's really cool."

She laughed. "That's good."

"It's very good."

She wrapped her arm around his waist as they walked down the sidewalk, heading for his car.

He veered her off in another direction. "Let's go for a walk. I like walking in the snow."

Oliver turned down a lane to cut across to where he knew there was a small park not far. When they reached it, Morgan's face lit up. The park was decorated for Christmas like a small wonderland. Oliver took her hand and pulled her down a path that was arched with lights. Even in daylight, it felt warm and special.

"It's beautiful here," Morgan said. "How did you know about this place?"

Oliver stopped and looked around. He knew

because he'd arranged it. He'd intended to bring her here that night, but he couldn't wait.

He turned and put a hand in his coat pocket. "Morgan. I — " He had a speech prepared, but as he looked at her, the attention that creased her forehead, her lips slightly puckered in wait for what he was about to say, his words dissolved. He wanted every part of her to be his, and he needed her to know it.

He pulled a small box from his pocket and held it up. "I love you more every day that we're together and I want you to be my wife." He lifted the lid of the box to show the single oval diamond set on a gold ring.

Her eyes widened and her lips separated into a surprised 'O'. She breathed out several puffs of frosty breath before responding, "Yes."

"You will?"

A smile filled her face. "Yes, I will."

He put the ring on her finger, then picked her up and twirled her around, feet crunching in the snow. He shouted up to the sky, unable to contain his joy.

Morgan laughed and kissed his neck before burying her face into it, squeezing her eyes tight. That they could reach this place and feel this joy after all the heartache was beyond belief.

She recalled the scriptures Lauren had showed her about Jesus returning for his bride and wondered if this was a glimpse of what he felt for his church. And that he would share it with her to experience in this moment was more than she would have ever hoped for.

Enjoy the book?

Book reviews are the most powerful tool I have as an author to grow my readership. If I had the sway of a New York publisher, perhaps it would be easier to gain attention, but a simple reader review is way better than what any top publisher can offer...

Readers like yourself are what make the biggest difference to an author, and if you've enjoyed this book and wouldn't mind spending a few minutes leaving a review, it would help me out immensely.

Free Novella

One of the best things about being a writer is that I get to build relationships with my readers. And one of the best ways to do that is through a newsletter. I'm not a prolific emailer, but I will occasionally send out a newsletter with details on new releases, special offers, other projects I've been working on and anything else I have that might be of interest.

When you sign up, you'll get the prequel to the Shadow Alliance Series, free. This prequel tells the story of Peter and Jemi and how they met.

GET YOUR FREE EBOOK NOW

Or visit pgturners.com

Also by Shawna Coleing

Shadow Alliance Series

Christian Romantic Suspense

SHADOW GAME (book 1)

SHADOW LINE (book 2)

SHADOW BREAK (book 3)

SHADOW TRACE (book 4)

SHADOW POINT (book 5)

Want more of Peter Black? Read Hidden Alliance…

Hidden Alliance Series

Christian Romantic Suspense

HIDDEN TRIAL (book 1)

HIDDEN ASCENT (book 2)

HIDDEN DEPTHS (book 3)

HIDDEN CHANCE (book 4)

Inspired by Judges Series

Contemporary Christian Romantic Suspense

SAMSON

GIDEON

JEP

JAEL

Underwood Series

Christian Thriller

UNDER THE VEIL (book 1)

UNDER FIRE (book 2)

UNDER SIEGE (book 3)

Bristol Kelley Duology

A clean romantic suspense

SLEIGHT OF HAND (book 1)

SMOKE AND MIRRORS (book 2)

Erin Hart Duology

A clean romantic suspense

OUT ON A LIMB (book 1)

CUT TO THE CHASE (book 2)

About the Author

Shawna Coleing is the author of the Shadow Alliance Series. You can find her on her website or feel free to contact her by email at:
shawnacoleing@pgturners.com

Otherwise you can connect with her here:

Acknowledgments

Always and forever, thanks to God for being who He says He is. To mum and dad who were my first biggest fans. To Tim for your encouragement and interest in my stories. To Matt and the kids for being interested in my passion to write. To Elizabeth Smith for your proof-reading skills and a bit extra. And to many friends who have been lifting me up on this journey. You've kept my spirits high when I was tired of the whole thing and made sure I didn't give up.

Made in the USA
Monee, IL
09 May 2026